P9-DDT-218

Each Night Was Illuminated

ALSO BY JODI LYNN ANDERSON

The Peaches Trilogy
Peaches
The Secrets of Peaches
Love and Peaches

Tiger Lily
The Vanishing Season
Midnight at the Electric

JODI LYNN ANDERSON

Each Night Was Illuminated

Quill Tree Books
An Imprint of HarperCollins Publishers

"To Those Born After", originally published in German in 1939 as
"An die Nachgeborenen", translated by Tom Kuhn. Copyright 1939,
© 1961 by Bertolt-Brecht-Erben / Suhrkamp Verlag. Translation
copyright © 2019, 2015 by Tom Kuhn and David Constantine,
from COLLECTED POEMS OF BERTOLT BRECHT by
Bertolt Brecht, translated by Tom Kuhn and David Constantine.
Used by permission of Liveright Publishing Corporation.

Quill Tree Books is an imprint of HarperCollins Publishers.

Each Night Was Illuminated
Copyright © 2022 by Jodi Lynn Anderson
All rights reserved. Printed in the United States of America.
No part of this book may be used or reproduced in any manner
whatsoever without written permission except in the case of
brief quotations embodied in critical articles and reviews. For
information address HarperCollins Children's Books, a division of
HarperCollins Publishers, 195 Broadway, New York, NY 10007.
www.epicreads.com

Library of Congress Control Number: 2022931762
ISBN 978-0-06-239357-9

Typography by Molly Fehr
22 23 24 25 26   PC/LSCH   10 9 8 7 6 5 4 3 2 1
❖
First Edition

T 18520

For Mark

AUTHOR'S NOTE

The character of Saint Eia in this novel is loosely based on historical accounts of Saint Ia of the Celts. I have taken many artistic liberties with her, however, and have therefore altered her name.

If you wish to rise, begin by descending.

—Saint Augustine

Prologue

TO PICTURE MANHATTAN IN THE FLOOD, you have to try to picture it like this: the city up to its knees in water, a back of bristled buildings rising in a river that's joined to the sea. I lie floating, fighting for my breath, and watch it come into view.

It's morning but not yet light, and even though it seems the city shouldn't have power, the lights of the skyscrapers glitter. Helicopters buzz around the skyline. I see the tiny dots of rescue boats glowing like beacons, dots of what might be people in the water. They are so small under the vast, approaching sky, the city a confluence of a million chaotic things, cobbled together and humming with life. I probably won't live to see what has survived.

I bob, catching mouthfuls of water, slipping. I will end up at the bottom of the Hudson River like all the gangsters. I will sleep with the fishes tonight. I want to make a joke about this to someone. The loneliness of knowing that I never will is crushing.

I float on the current and keep my eyes on the lights as if they could stop me from sinking. I think about the few small words that brought me here.

"Close your eyes," Elias said, doing that up-and-down thing he does, that restless slight bouncing on the balls of his feet that made him look eight and not eighteen. "Think about our secrets. The things only you and me were there for."

And when I look back to the things only he and I were there for, I realize for the first time how they are all water-bound: a night it snowed in summer, a train in a lake, a boy in a river. I have a mermaid destiny, it seems.

It makes me think about Saint Eia. She, too, had to face the water. Her faith made a leaf grow to fit her and float her home across the sea.

And then the hairs stand up on my neck and my eyelids quiver and I see them, so tiny and distant, up around the spires of the Chrysler Building and soaring above the peak of the Freedom Tower. They flutter in the dying wind, the quieting storm, buffeted by a swirl of clouds so wide they look like they might be battered down out of the air.

I'm imagining them, of course. Still, they circle the sky, steadily doing their work.

I know it's all in my head. But still, I want so badly to reach them.

I don't believe in them. But the dead have come for me anyway.

Part
1

Chapter 1

I WAS ALWAYS TRYING TO LOSE ELIAS, FROM the moment I met him. I knew him for less than two hours that first time. But it was enough to entangle us for life.

It was a hot, green summer; I was eleven. That afternoon I was standing under the KISS tree with a bunch of other kids my age. We were all circled on our bikes, arguing with Peter Murphy about penises.

The thread of Peter's argument went something like this: girls couldn't climb as high as boys, thanks to boys having penises (though the middle of the argument, where the link between penises and tree-scaling ability was established, was fuzzy). And that's why, Peter claimed, the name of his crush, a girl from our class named Wendy McGowan, was now carved majestically at least eight feet off the ground. (The KISS tree being where you carved the names of people you wanted to kiss; the higher the name the more passionate the love.)

Things like this had been raging all summer, about girls and boys and what we were and weren't capable of. "Just look at God," Peter said. "He's the one in charge and does he have a penis or not?"

Standing astraddle my bike in a bathing suit, sputtering swear words at him half under my breath, I gazed at Peter's perfect eyelashes. I'd noticed he was always at his most confident when he didn't know what he was talking about, but I didn't care. All I could think about was what it would feel like to put my lips on his. Up till then I'd only had a crush on Finn in *Star Wars*, so it was a new and intoxicating feeling to even think about what kissing might be like.

It was also confusing, since I was planning to be a nun. Deeply religious, I was wearing a crucifix that my mom had left in a drawer, and a guardian angel bracelet I'd bought at the Mary Immaculate Fall Fling, but in my shorts pocket I also kept a rock that Peter had dropped once on the playground. The kids called me the Loch Ness Monster because I was so quiet you barely knew I existed, but I was also dangerous. Ever since my mom had left our family half a year earlier to move to Cleveland, I'd started pinching people who made me mad without ever saying a word, making blood rise up under their skin in welts.

Now I stood staring at the knife Peter dangled before us, having an inner battle, pride and anger making my heart skitter around like a moth. I knew I could climb the tree higher than he could, but not with people watching. And anyway, I knew proving Peter wrong about the penises would turn him against me and he'd never kiss me at all. I wanted to be the kind of girl Peter kissed. So I made a face of agreement that yes, girls could not climb.

That's when Elias ran past in shorts and a Coke T-shirt.

We studiously ignored him as we had all summer. The rest of us had known each other all our lives, but Elias was only visiting, and there was nothing like a true outsider to make you feel like an insider.

Every day, Elias ran laps of the neighborhood, but I'd never talked with him. He stood out in every possible way: thick wavy black hair that had a mind of its own—sometimes standing left and sometimes right but always strikingly determined as hair went. Brown skin among our sea of freckled pinks and tans, and when he talked, an accent that sounded like stretching out on the beach on a hot day. He was visiting from Australia, which—so far as we knew—was a dry place on the other side of the world with koalas, the world's deadliest spiders, and, of course, kangaroos.

He was here for the summer visiting his aunt and uncle, the Khans, who ran a bakery called Cookie Caverns one town over. You couldn't *completely* ignore him; he was too lean, tall, wiry, confident, his head always cocked like he was listening to some distant radio tuned to something interesting that wasn't us. Now he nodded to us with little interest, and we side-eyed him until he'd run past. We went on circling the tree and Peter went on pointing triumphantly at *Wendy McGowan*.

And then a voice boomed down the street summoning one of us for dinner, and we scattered like pool balls. Peter buried the knife in the dirt before leaving, clearly thinking it was a cool gesture. Soon even my sister, Thea, was gone, and it was only me left at the base of the tree, staring up at Wendy McGowan's name.

Once everyone was out of sight, I knelt in the dirt and dug out the knife. After a moment, in spite of my subpar vagina, I began to climb.

With long, strong legs, I scaled the tree fast; I knew Peter climbed like a sloth in comparison. Up past Wendy McGowan's name, I took in the view of the river rushing by and for the first time felt afraid. Dear God, watch over me, I thought. Dear Virgin Mary, watch over me. (My life was a litany of prayers—for As, safety, beauty.)

I turned to the tree and bit my lip, grasping the knife to carve. But something froze my hand. It was the idea of leaving a trace of myself that everyone would see.

I hesitated another moment, and then—instead of carving Peter's name—I kissed the tree, long and hard. I pulled back and looked out at the river and thought about making my way down. When my eyes skimmed the ground again, Elias Jones was watching me.

He was leaning to the left, hand at his side as if he had a cramp, panting from his run, his hair leaning left.

That's when I lost my balance and my grasp, and slid the rest of the way down, the bark scraping my legs. I landed on my back with a thud at his feet.

I bit my lip and looked down at my legs, a long, thin

cut seeping across my knee. We both gazed down at it, tiny and already clotting, but possibly, in my eyes, deadly.

"You okay?" Elias asked, the two words rolling out wide and friendly. I didn't meet his eyes.

"Yep." I hopped up and started walking home.

Elias, not one to be easily deterred, kept up a few feet behind me.

"You could pass out from blood loss," he said. "I'll make sure you get home without dying."

"I'm good."

Elias kept following me. He didn't seem to mind absolute rejection. And then an idea seemed to come to him; maybe he spotted my crucifix. "There's a spot on Cub Mountain where you can see heaven," he said.

That got my attention. I looked back at him. His face was creased with genuine worry, mixed with the curiosity of a boy who'd just seen a girl kiss a tree.

"Where?" I asked.

Our town was in full splendor that afternoon, the low hills green and lush, the old stone houses of downtown gray against the trees as we climbed. From up high we could see spires of my school's church, the cluster of brick buildings nestled among the woods. I wanted to take it all in as we walked, but Elias wouldn't stop talking.

"That's porcelain berry; it's invasive, did you know that? Did you know vines travel, just differently than people do? Did you know they put out their little feelers and pat around like mimes before they climb? At the farm my dad works we have this tree called a boab"—the vowels stretched out, *bowaab*—"that looks like a joke. It used to freak me out because I thought it was from another planet. My aunty loves them; she has bad hair. She has this huge mole on her cheek; I feel bad for her because she hates it; I guess I hate it for her too. I could get a boab seed and mail it to you, even though it's probably against the law . . . just give me your address. You don't talk much," he said. To which I did not respond. Elias went on.

I listened but pretended not to. Elias liked nature, *a lot*. And movies. He loved to run. (He seemed to like everything except his aunt's mole.) His grandmother was from Bangladesh, but she fell madly in love with and married an Australian farmer when she immigrated. His dad was mostly a farmer but had done all sorts of jobs over the years: fruit picking, plucking pearls from oysters. As he chattered on, I watched the houses grow smaller below us and felt myself getting farther and farther from home, which was thrilling but also scary. Since my mom had left, I'd gotten cautious. I didn't know why then, but I think when your own mom leaves you in the dust, you start watching the world closer to see what else might surprise you. Not that my mom had ever been a full-on mom anyway: her leaving had only confirmed she'd been half gone all along.

Finally, out of breath, Elias announced, "We're here."

We perched on a boulder at the top of the mountain. From this spot you could see the reservoir that doubled as our town's only lake, the bridge that cut across it for passing trains, the Green Valley River below it, and the giant old-fashioned hotel—the Rose—that had perched along its craggy bank almost since the town was born. A train was moving slowly in Green Valley's direction, like a silver caterpillar inching its way toward Reservoir Bridge. It was a lucky sighting; the line had fallen out of use because of quicker routes.

But what grabbed my attention was the toylike view of New York City east of us. It was a tiny skyline in the distance, twenty or so miles away but unmistakable: a hazy gray cluster of buildings stretching skyward, as unreachable and imaginary to me as the Emerald City of Oz. The adults of Green Valley traveled there all the time—to work, to hang out, to visit friends—but for kids like me, it was an elusive place. It felt like the center of gravity around which our town revolved, and also like another planet.

The one thing missing from the view was heaven.

I was starting to think I'd been duped. Elias squinted at the sky, at two puffy white clouds making their slow way over us. "I guess you can only see it on a clear day," he said. I'd realize, when I knew him again years later, that he always squinted when he lied.

He seemed to be thinking of some way to distract me. He looked at me but avoided my eyes, and then his gaze traveled to my hand. I realized I'd forgotten to put the knife down when we left the tree.

But that wasn't what he was looking at. He reached out and touched a finger lightly to my bracelet. I held it out for him to see: the charm adorned with a tiny holy scene: it was a famous image of a guardian angel following two innocent and rather clueless kids as they crossed a treacherous, rushing stream while she floated behind them—unseen but powerfully protective. I loved it, and I believed in it. I felt like if I wore the bracelet, the angel would follow me around too, hovering near my bed, making sure all was well.

Elias peered at it, his eyebrows low and intent. "She

looks like she's hiding something," he said dubiously. I frowned at the angel, perplexed, searching for what he saw. And then he slipped the knife from my hand.

"I have an idea," he said. "I saw this in a movie." He bit his lip and—too quickly for me to process what he was doing or react—sliced a long thin line into his palm. Then he pushed his palm against the cut on my knee and smiled before pulling his hand away. My heart pounded for a moment.

He shrugged. "There, we're blood siblings now."

I blinked, shocked by his foolhardiness. I wanted to tell him it didn't really count, but didn't have the heart.

"I was just going to carve my own name on the tree," I lied, the first full sentence I'd said to him. He studied me, and maybe he believed me or not.

"I leave tomorrow for Australia," he said. "But if you give me your address, I promise I'll write. Like, real letters, not messaging." He waited for me to agree. "Letters are more mysterious," he added.

I shrugged. I was kind of enjoying Elias's enthusiastic and constant chatter, but I felt I'd be giving up all my power by showing it. And then I spelled out my address for him, figuring he wouldn't remember. We sat in silence for a while, watching the train wind its way through the edges of town and onto the bridge over the lake.

I was half daydreaming about Peter Murphy's lips and getting home before I got in trouble when it happened.

The valley must have echoed the sound of it . . . because before I saw it, I *heard* it. It was the scrape and scream of metal first that made us jerk. A *wrong* sound, a gut punch kind of sound even from a distance.

My eyes were on the train in the valley before I knew why. The train lurched strangely leftward. The scrape became a shriek, the sound of metal howling. And then the half of the train that had crossed onto the bridge *slumped*. Screams tore from the windows as both bridge and train sagged, making my skin crawl and my heart thud sickly. And then, in an echo of metal, a piece of Reservoir Bridge vanished underneath itself, like a nightmare. Half the train cars crashed into the dark water with it.

I didn't make a sound. All my terror went in instead of out, a curling knot of knives in my chest. At some point I hadn't noticed, Elias had gripped my arm, and now he dug his fingers deep into my skin. Moments passed and felt eternal. And then came a silence, as if, for a terrifying moment, no one but us had noticed. Like we were the only ones who could save the people trapped underwater, which of course, we weren't. And then came the sirens and the screams of the people above.

And what could we do, the two of us, but watch?

Moments passed as the lights of fire trucks and ambulances and police cars descended on the valley, and then I felt Elias's fingers jerk again and clutch me tighter, as if something new had happened. And he said something strange then—something that would seem stranger in the years that came after.

"Do you see them?" he asked.

I thought for a moment, hopefully, he meant people must be swimming up to the surface from the submerged cars. I looked for the shapes of them making their escape. But no one was there.

Later, I'd think he was only hoping . . . and asking me to confirm his hope. But that, too, would turn out to be wrong.

"We'd better go," I said.

We walked home down the mountain, stunned, while the sounds of sirens still echoed through the trees. We didn't talk. Adults, distraught and loud, were gathered in a gaggle on my block when we emerged from the woods at the end of Woodland. My dad was among them, talking to Mrs. Christopoulos from across the street. Nobody noticed us, or that we'd been gone at all.

And, in the way of children who don't know what they *can* and can't be blamed for, we said nothing about what we'd seen. We'd been where we shouldn't . . . and seen something terrible we shouldn't have seen.

I heard about it later on the news. A weakness in the short spans, rusted by something in the water, had made the bridge collapse. Six people died that day in the accident over the reservoir: the conductor and the only passengers in the forward car. The passengers were all in the same family . . . the family that owned the Rose Hotel. They were returning from a trip to the city: the mom and dad, two teenage daughters, and one teenage son. Luckily, the other cars had been empty.

We were a wiry, curious boy and a Loch Ness Monster of a girl just exploring the woods toward the borders of our small and quiet world. We had seen something there were no words for. And so, we wouldn't know, until many years later, how we had seen something completely different.

Our secrets had only just begun.

Dear Cassie, Elias wrote, nearly a month after he'd gone back to Australia, though I'd never expected to hear from him again. The envelope was addressed politely to *Ms. Cassie Blake. I wish that we could talk in person. I need to ask you something private.*

And then, weeks later,

> *Dear Cassie,*
> *The priests are wrong, God doesn't have a penis—God is an eight-armed destructor named Ganesha and she has huge boobs and, boy, is she pissed. I learned this from my great-aunty's best friend from Bangladesh, who's Hindu. Anyway, I thought you'd be happy about that.*
> *Things are bad on the farm. We are waiting for rain.*

> *Dear Cassie,*
> *A volcano erupted and nearly crashed a plane, can you imagine? Just think, millions of years, civilizations and countries and fast food come along, and the internet, and you end up in your business suit in the sky in a LAVA CLOUD, like you are a pterodactyl*

*or something, like you might as well not be modern at
all. I've been watching Lord of the Rings and there's
a volcano in that too. Only I just like the Shire parts,
which are there to make the Orcs look extra crappy for
destroying everything. My dad says the best way to win
people over is to ask them about themselves. So where
do you stand on Orcs?*

Dear Cassie,

*I thought when you said I could write you, you
would write me back. Are you writing me back? We are
brother and sister, after all. Hardy har.*

Dear Cassie,

*I'm worried about some things. If you write to me,
I'll tell you more. The suspense! It's killing you!*

Dear Cassie,

*I kissed a girl. Have you ever kissed anyone? Any
pointers, ha ha? Things are bad on the farm. Like,
really bad. So much has dried up. Write back.*

I read Elias's letters in a distracted way for the next couple of years, but I did not keep them or reply. I couldn't

really say why not, except that I didn't like to think of the day of the train, and the two could not be separated.

And so, when the letters stopped abruptly somewhere in year three, I barely noticed. I grew and somewhere I guessed he did, too, if I thought about him at all.

Meanwhile, the day of the train had taken two things from me. My belief that anything in this world was safe and my belief in God.

I'd watched six people die a horrible death, and it had torn open a seam in what I thought I knew. In that moment, even as a kid, it had suddenly all seemed so cut and dry: people were there and then they were un-there. No *Surprise! Actually, you have earned eternal life!* No great being making things right, or even there at all.

I prayed desperately to be proven wrong, every night, for years. I asked hard things from God for proof that He existed: Please make that car fly. Please make it snow in summer. When that didn't work, I asked for less and less: Please make that bird land on that branch right . . . now. Please make that person turn their head to the left.

But it didn't work. God had leaked out of me like air from a tire, dispersing into the atmosphere, irretrievable.

When I heard about Australia or the Great Barrier Reef or the Glass House Mountains that were leftover plugs of volcanoes, it was a cartoon place and Elias was a cartoon boy who lived there—far from my mind and getting further all the time. The whole world was somehow less real than Green Valley and also dangerous.

And then years later, Elias reappeared.

Once he did, we would know each other for seventy-eight days. There would be a clock on us, from the start.

It began, of course, with a letter.

Chapter 2

IT LANDED IN OUR MAILBOX IN THE LATE spring of my senior year of high school, on a morning after I'd been up all night.

Somewhere around the time I'd turned seventeen, I'd stopped sleeping. Or rather, I slept only two or three hours a night and then crashed every few days, only to start the process again. There was nothing to trigger this sleeplessness, though we looked for it, and therapists and doctors and my family tried their best to fix me. I tried Ambien and trazodone and Lunesta . . . valerian root, meditating, juice fasts, and melatonin. But for whatever reason, none of it worked. It was like my body suddenly forgot how to cross that line between sleep and wakefulness. It would get to the edge of sleep but hardly ever swam for it.

When you're sleep-deprived all the time, you have to keep moving like a shark to make it through the day; it's like you have to keep moving to breathe. Also, you're always half dreaming. You think you're holding a pen in your hand and look down to find there was never any pen; you remember putting your books in your bag only to find you left them on your desk. I once was so delirious I thought a zebra rug abandoned by the highway had escaped from the zoo.

The morning the letter arrived, I'd spent the night as usual: blinking at nothing until the day slowly lightened, revealing a low gray cloud cover that had been with us since December. I'd gotten up at the crack of dawn with my little brother, Gabe.

An ad for Noxzema was on the TV in the kitchen, showing a girl intermittently washing her face and having a great life as a result. It was the kind of ad that suddenly made you wonder if there wasn't something a little wrong with the skin on your face. I was making Gabe's lunch as I watched.

"I don't want my cherry tomatoes chopped," he said, watching me. Just two early birds, me and Gabe.

"They're a choking hazard."

Gabe sighed. I thought everything was a choking hazard: grapes, hot dogs, ice cubes, popcorn. I liked to crumble Gabe's popcorn when he wasn't looking so it would be safer.

I was about to go down the list for him of the world's choking hazards anyway just to make sure he knew what to look out for, when Dad appeared, already dressed in the "everyman" style he wore at Chevrolet, where he sold cars. "Thea's not up yet?" he asked.

"Why leave the boudoir?" I said, nodding in the direction of my older sister's cavernous bedroom above, full of silk comforters, hoarded chocolate, and the world's most intense home nail bar. She'd sleep until ten at least. My dad poured some coffee and adjusted to being awake. The Noxzema ad had ended, and now on the news a bunch of guys in suits were meeting about something involving the fate of the world.

I goosed the back of Gabe's neck before laying a bowl of Cheerios in front of him. (You can't choke on Cheerios; I'd looked it up.) Gabe immediately stuck a Cheerio in his ear, then made two others fight each other to the death, tossing them into an imaginary abyss, and then crawled onto my lap, breathing his sweet morning breath on me and curling against my chest. My brother had two settings: pure sociopathic barbarity and Mother Teresa–level sweetness.

My dad took one more glance at the TV as he gulped his coffee. "Can you check the mail on your way out? And if my check for overtime is there, can you deposit it?"

He took Gabe's hand and they disappeared out the door. "Light a candle for your mom since you'll be over there," Dad said. I nodded. Mom still lived in Cleveland with a guy she'd married, but—except for the first year or so after she left, when she'd call from time to time—we never talked. I never lit candles for her. I doubted she lit candles for us.

I was sleepy and dazed when I pulled everything out of the mailbox, so I didn't really notice it: the scrawled handwriting, the foreign postmark, the dusty feel of it, as if it had been mailed directly from a sunbaked place. I stuffed it into my backpack.

By the time I'd started the car, the letter had vanished from my mind.

I wound my ancient Pontiac, littered with Thea's Vitamin-water bottles and gum wrappers, through downtown. You couldn't throw a rock in Green Valley without hitting a church, but the one I was aiming for was the sprawling Sisters of the Holy Redeemer campus on the other side of town. It was far out, a drive that included a distant view of the increasingly shabby Rose Hotel across the river, a rocky outcropping called Chimney Rise reaching up behind it like a crooked finger.

As I pulled into the parish hall driveway, a statue of the Virgin Mary opened her hands out to me, looking vaguely disappointed. Behind her, at the front doors, Sister Suzanne, my favorite nun, was waiting impatiently.

"I have a crap ton of work for you today," she said as I climbed out of my car. She smiled wryly at me. I could tell she'd already had plenty of coffee, nuns getting up almost as early as insomniacs.

She led me through room after room with her signature impatient, heavy-footed tread. We cut through the sacristy, lined with gold fabric and framed paintings of the Virgin Mary and photos of our bishop. Finally we reached an empty stone-walled room with piles of books all over the floor.

"They were willed to us by one of the parishioners who just died—very wealthy lady, her house has more antiques than the Met. They just came in Tuesday." Sister Suzanne had created a parish library years ago and put out a call for religious books of all sorts. "It's quite a collection, a lot on the Dark Ages." She nodded to the books, which had titles like *Pagan Britain* and *The Growth of Mysticism, Hildegard of Bingen*, and *The Rule of Saint Benedict*. I laid the books aside and picked up another with a plain black cover and a gold embossed title: *Saint Eia of the Celts*. The pages were yellowed but legible. The type was tiny and the book was thick enough to be a doorstop, but I tended to see this quality in books as a kind of personal dare.

"That one's rare. There aren't many Dark Age saints we know of. So few records left behind—that's why they call them Dark Ages." I flipped through the book in my hands. It was full of faded illustrations of Celts in the woods, men in armor carrying crosses that glowed with godly light. It felt instantly mysterious, like something unearthed by Indiana Jones.

"Nothing for the faint of heart about betting your whole life on God," Sister Suzanne liked to say, but I was unconvinced. I loved the safety of the convent: the incense-scented halls, the quiet cave-like stillness. It made me *still* secretly want to be a nun, despite the minor inconvenience of not believing in anything. Plus Sister Suzanne was a badass, and the convent paid me surprisingly well . . . though I supposed nuns themselves weren't exactly raking it in.

"This is your job," Sister Suzanne said, nodding around the room. "Start organizing, cataloging."

I looked around. "Can't wait."

"Nerd." Sister Suzanne sighed, because she knew I was not being sarcastic. I liked organizing things neatly the way some people liked parties.

After another look around at the enormous task, she lifted her hands. "It'll take a couple weeks, probably." And then, helplessly, "Thanks, Cass." With that, she vanished, leaving me alone with the dusty room and the quiet.

I sat on the floor and flipped through a few more books before getting started. A lot of them were illustrated with lithographs and watercolor prints—some quite gruesomely—with beheadings, upside-down crucifixions, hearts on fire for Christ. Somehow, though, browsing them felt cozy. I guess time puts such distance between things that even upside-down crucifixions take on a layer of quaintness after a while. Maybe the comforting and cozy thing is that it happened but it was over. Or that it happened but you yourself are safe and warm, kind of like sitting indoors when it's raining.

I turned back to the book about Saint Eia, which was by far the most interesting of the bunch. There was a foreword that included a poem by Bertolt Brecht, a German writer who'd lived in exile during World War II—a bloodthirsty, warlike poem that seemed kind of weird at the beginning of a holy book. A plate at the front gave a brief description of the saint: a Celtic warrior princess who left home at fifteen in pursuit of a precious relic stolen from her tribe. In the process she converted to Christianity and crossed an ocean on a leaf that, thanks to her faith, grew to fit her. How she died, it didn't say.

I felt envy, flipping through her story. My dad liked to talk about the challenges of faith, but to me it seemed like it must be the nicest thing in the world to think this really perfect bearded dude was taking care of everybody's business somewhere.

I slipped the book into my backpack to borrow, and then set about organizing the space.

Time flew. I spent the bulk of the morning and half of the afternoon making headway, only breaking for lunch with the sisters.

I'd forgotten I even had the letter until that night when, unpacking, I saw it among the pile of things on my bed. And this time, now that I really looked, a quiver went through me a moment before my mind caught up. I recognized the handwriting in the strange way people have of recognizing two notes of a song, like you know it before you *know* it.

> *Dear Cassie,*
> *I'm coming back to town in late May and would really like to ask you something. Call me?*

He'd written down his number at the bottom.

I felt my face flush with the memory of the train sinking into the lake. Which was still a secret, for no logical reason I could explain. I suppose childhood lies sometimes carry into adulthood long after it makes sense.

I read the letter a couple more times, then folded it up.

That night I lay awake in the heat.

We had no AC and, despite it being early spring, the

heat was already sticky because of the constant dampness. I had my window wide open to get whatever stilted breeze I could as, wide-eyed, I stared at the walls. I had a habit at night of thinking of things going wrong in the world: floods, hurricanes, tornadoes, Big Oil, wind power, infighting among my favorite reality TV stars.

I remembered, vaguely, the other letters from when we were kids. What had Elias's life been like since I knew him? What had happened to him while I'd been living in this same quiet town every year? What did he want to talk about? I pictured the farm and its many cows and Elias riding a horse across a wide-open, sunburned space, a piece of the world that felt as far away as it was possible to go.

The letter was a messy thing landing in my careful life. And I didn't want anything to do with it. Not Elias's mysterious question. Not his strangerness, his other-side-of-the-worldness. Not his longing to connect.

Eventually I lay watching the sun come up, that familiar boundless space in my chest. And by then I'd decided that Elias Jones could have nothing to say to me that I would want to hear.

If I was drowning, I didn't yet know it. If the tectonic plates of my life were shifting, I was sure it was the opposite: everything tidy, careful, right in its place.

And so I set out to ignore him a second time.

Weeks passed and I began to think he wasn't coming back after all.

But he did come back. And when he did, as it turns out, I was the one who went after *him*.

Chapter 3

A FEW WEEKS AFTER I RECEIVED ELIAS'S strange letter, long after I'd put it out of mind, he resurfaced through, of all people, my sister, Thea.

We were at church. It was postgraduation, early June and hot and crowded, mostly because of something that had come to be known as *Le Tits Now*. The church was packed that Sunday: not to see boobs but because we'd all seen them, and some people want to *unsee* them . . . and it made for a good turnout.

Basically, the night before Christmas last year, some teenagers had tampered with the manger scene in front of the church, spacing out the letters of LET IT SNOW beside the nativity to spell LE TITS NOW. They'd also given Mary a jaunty beret.

Any other year, it would have been forgotten as the cry of suburban boredom it was, but lately the town had been combustible, mostly I guess because the whole world had gotten combustible. The Le Tits Now nativity scene turned out to be like a match dropped in dry tinder. And all it had taken was a few months for Father James Copper to blow the flames into a fire.

Father James had been buzzing around Green Valley almost as long as I could remember, railing against his favorite topics, which, in descending order, were: emotional-needs service animals, Whole Foods, and—for some reason I could never make heads or tails of—Hawaiian Punch.

An angry, pinched, unlikable man, he'd been foisted on us from a parish in Upstate New York that didn't want him, a tactic we hoped to replicate someday. It had even become a local phrase: to *Father James* someone was to slip away from an annoying person at a gathering as soon as someone else joined the conversation.

He was the kind of guy who read something once on Facebook and, as long as it made him feel offended, posted it a thousand times without ever following up on the source. While Father Bob and Father Eric spent a lot of their sermons talking about how to walk in light and love thy neighbor, Father James was more focused on the idea that God would separate the sheep from the goats, and the goats were basically people who disagreed with him.

Lacking in any healthy level of self-doubt (I tend to think a decent person should doubt themselves at least 20 percent), he was drawn to conspiracy theories like a moth to a flame. Thea swore—though nobody else had ever corroborated it—that he once told her third-grade class that Big Agriculture had invented a chicken with two butts but only one head because it made more meat. I didn't know if she was telling the truth, but it did make me wonder if the seminary was having low matriculation the year that they'd accepted him.

Still, as unlikable as he was, he did have a certain charm. He loved dogs and dogs loved him, and he could compliment the heck out of old ladies. It was this weird kind of reverse charisma: small, nice things he did stood out because he was so rarely nice. And then Le Tits Now had put him on the map.

In the Mary Immaculate community there were two kinds of Catholics: the-eye-for-an-eye ones and the turn-the-other-cheek ones. The eye-for-an-eye ones were all about the price of sin and the turn-the-other-cheek ones liked to buy cage-free eggs and thought everything was up for debate, including the existence of hell.

Given that, on the town's social media page, schisms could form around decaf versus regular, Le Tits Now had been explosive. And given that, in Father James's view, boobs were already pretty much sins in and of themselves because a lot of guys couldn't stop staring at them (and therefore it must be the boobs' fault), it was like he'd thrown a saddle on all that anger and ridden it into the spotlight: the prank wasn't just a prank, it was *them* hating *us* (though who *they* were, I don't know, because the guys who did it were a couple of assholes in my senior class at Mary Immaculate).

Father James was good at convincing people that any group he didn't like could be defined by their jackasses alone. I think some people were so hurt by Le Tits Now they wanted to believe him. And so, the same way you can't stop worrying a loose tooth once you notice it, suddenly, inexplicably, people had been showing up at his sermons that had always been empty before—in a way they never did for sweet, gentle Father Bob, who talked about forgiveness and always let people go home early to get ready for the Super Bowl. And, in the nonsensical way you can only find in real life, it had all somehow led to the current war over the Skyline View construction project.

Long story short, a contractor was building a huge cluster of houses on Cub Mountain. It was bringing jobs and money to Green Valley, but it was also tearing up half the mountain's trees. Some engineers were saying that was *too many* trees, because—with thousands of roots gone—all the dirt from the mountain would run into the reservoir.

You wouldn't think something so boring could be a huge controversy, but in Father James's world everything you could disagree on was basically war. People wanted jobs and at the same time, people also didn't want the reservoir to overflow. But according to Father James, two opposite things couldn't be true at the same time. So the people who opposed Skyline View *cared more about trees than people*. Also, they hated our town and, worse, they *hated America*.

I looked around, wondering why everyone wasn't

laughing. Thea was posting selfies on her feed while my eyes roved to a bird who'd flown in and gotten trapped, praying God would prove me wrong about His existence by having the bird crap on Father James's head.

"Their wine is the venom of snakes, and the deadly poison of cobras," Father James said, gripping his lectern. He was fond of quoting Deuteronomy. He went on about how man was supposed to fill the earth and subdue it while the word *snakes* rattled around inside me like a warning. I wondered if there was a way to mark our doors with lamb's blood to indicate that we wholeheartedly supported construction projects and were to be spared if the Skyline View zombie apocalypse came.

Beside me, Thea paused her fingers on her phone, staring at a photo.

"That Australian kid is back," she whispered. "He got hot."

My blood seemed to freeze. I looked down at my hands to avoid her eyes, the hairs standing up along the back of my neck. She thrust her phone into my line of sight to show me the post she was looking at.

The photo was low-res; it was all blurry and grainy and poorly lit, like a photo you might see of a UFO in a tabloid: an image both elusive and nefarious. But I'd recognize him anywhere, even with the years that had passed: opinionated hair, wiry, his shoulders a little too big for the rest of him. My body reacted to the memory of the train, flaming up with the secrecy of it, and the curiosity about his letter that I'd stuffed deep inside myself.

"What's with the bad photo?" I asked.

"Kelsey's seen him three times, on the surveillance video of their driveway. It's weird; he walks the neighborhood late at night. He carries all these bags around and some kind of laser thing. She was wondering if she should call the cops. Rumor is his parents sent him here because he was wanted in Sydney for burglary."

Gabe, sitting on the other side of me, picking his boogers, nudged me. Father James had noticed us whispering. Deficient as he was in the de-escalating conflict department, the priest had the eyes of an eagle, and the only thing he hated more than Hawaiian Punch was people not hanging on to his words like he was Jesus's true and only representative on earth. Hands on the lectern, he had clamped his mouth closed, and we shut up.

Thea put down her phone, and we tried to look attentive for the rest of the sermon. Afterward, we waited for

35

the church to empty out so Gabe could attempt to free the uncooperative bird who hadn't shit on Father James's head after all.

That night, I saw on the news that a glacier had broken away from Antarctica, the footage stark and haunting. They cut to footage of activists from a group called One World that literally hand-rescued turtles and painted slogans on sides of buildings like No Earth, No Birth. Today they were blocking traffic in San Francisco to call attention to climate change.

"Do you think the world's going to end?" I asked my dad.

"Oh brother," Thea replied for him, sitting at the table scrolling through her phone.

"What *oh brother*?"

"These are the same people who rescue chickens." I looked at her. Ever since we were kids Thea had been like this—suspicious of anything "weird," which was basically anything that made her uncomfortable. I didn't know if it had started before my mom left or after, but whatever the reason, Thea dismissed things beyond Green Valley's orbit easily. I looked to my dad, who seemed satisfied with this explanation.

"Don't let them bother you, Cass."

Whenever I worried about these things, my dad liked to repeat the Bible verse "Not a single sparrow can fall to the ground without your Father knowing it." Which meant, basically, that God held the world in His hands. I thought but didn't say that he might feel differently if he were a polar bear standing on an ice sheet drifting nowhere. But I thought a lot of things I didn't say when it came to my family.

I hadn't told them about my nonbelieving, all these years. My dad was a deacon. We still had a statue of Saint Joseph buried in the front yard from when we once tried to sell the house, and my aunt was a nun in Yonkers. You could say that I was in too deep with God to ever be out. Still, I tried to let Dad's words settle my stomach. I liked to believe him because he was usually right about things. But he also believed in heaven, so it was like he had a backup plan, which was an unfair advantage.

Anyway, I'd be living in Green Valley until I was old and dead anyway, far from the ice caps and therefore maybe safe from their demise. In the fall, I was going to a college only twenty minutes away, the same as Thea. I'd still be living at home, like she did. As Gabe's only non-mom mom, I needed to be close to take care of him, to bombard him with love, to keep him safe. Thea was more like a *real* older sister to him, just kind of generally annoyed by him, and she didn't crumble his popcorn and chop his cherry tomatoes like I did. I was the one who made sure his three pet gerbils didn't starve, that he wore his bike helmet, and that he was generally okay. Graduating had changed just about nothing for me. Which was the way I preferred it.

That night, I shook off my fear from the news by ironing my clothes and organizing my room, sweeping lint off the rugs, and rubbing the dust off my ill-advised and creepy collection of porcelain horses I'd had since childhood, which I was too nostalgic to get rid of. I put Gabe to bed with exactly three stories, because routine calmed him and me both. Then, when everyone else in the house was asleep, I turned to my book about Saint Eia.

Her people, the Celts, believed in gods and goddesses living in bushes and in trees, hidden under hills, in the foam of waterfalls. At Mary Immaculate we learned that Christians had brought the light of Jesus to pagans. But in this book, the pagans sounded rather magical on their own: they looked everywhere in nature and saw a holy thing.

Nevertheless, the Dark Ages being what they were, the Celts got violently, horrifically raided by the Saxons. And in addition to killing a bunch of people, the Saxons took the pride and joy of Saint Eia's tribe: a golden stone said to allow its holder to speak with the dead. Off the Saxons went in the direction of Rome, burning everything in their wake.

At the end of the chapter I was reading, Saint Eia set off after them into the vast unknown of the European continent, to get the golden stone back and bust some heads with her spear.

I settled back against my pillow, looking at the time on my phone: 2:15.

And then I noticed it: the slow, shallow breathing close by, a tiny sliding of socks against carpet.

"I know you're there," I said. "Can't sleep?"

Gabe had hidden himself at the foot of the bed. He fancied himself to be something of a ninja.

"How'd all the snakes get into our town?" he whispered, emerging from his hiding spot.

My heart crunched. I gave his shirt a tug and he climbed into my bed.

"He was talking about bad guys, not real snakes," I

said. Sometimes, almost all the time, I didn't know how to answer Gabe's questions. After knowing him a brief six years, I'd realized the world most certainly did not deserve him, or any little kid really.

Gabe's eyes widened and he sucked in a surprised breath. "Bad guys are *real*?" he whispered to me, like I'd just confirmed the existence of unicorns.

Crap. I backpedaled.

"They're not even bad guys, they're just people. Father James is full of shit, Gabe." There were times I wished Gabe had a real mom around instead of me. I got everything at least 25 percent wrong.

I let him snuggle into me and smelled the top of his head, which to me smelled better than cake. Loving Gabe was a sensory experience. Sometimes you had to remind yourself that he only reached up to your waist, he took up so much room in life.

"Do you believe me?"

He nodded. But sometimes Gabe just lied to make people feel better about making *him* feel better. The kid thought nothing was funnier than saying the word *fart-butt*, but he also contained multitudes.

After taking him back to his room, I stood and looked out my window at the overcast, drizzly night. I feared things, a low hum I couldn't name. I was awake and lonely and deeply unsettled, and somewhere glaciers were breaking away from continents. *And,* if the rumors were to be believed, Elias Jones was at this very moment roaming the streets of Green Valley doing something possibly menacing. I needed something and I didn't know what: to get out of this room, this brain that wouldn't sleep.

In the hall, I put on my rain jacket and snuck out of the house and walked in the direction of Elias's street. A light drizzle—more of a mist that frizzed my hair—gathered all over me in little drops. It was 3:00 a.m. by now, but I'd only walked two hundred yards when I bumped into Elias himself.

Chapter 4

HE WAS DRESSED LIKE A CAT BURGLAR FROM a sixties movie, all in black, and holding some weird equipment just as Thea had described. In his left hand was some kind of red laser, which, in the moment I spotted him, was pointing at the roof of our neighbors, the Christopouloses. In his right, he clasped a little yellow box that flashed a laser pattern across me as he turned at my approach.

I stumbled back as Elias stepped toward me in the dark, covering me in laser lights.

Several moments of confusion and silence passed before he spoke.

"Cassie?"

In the misty glow coming from the streetlamp I could see his face dimly now. He was tall, strikingly tall. I wondered how he recognized me.

"Hey, Elias," I said, flaming with guilt and embarrassment. I gestured to his height, to cover my confusion. "What have they been feeding you in Australia?"

"What are you doing out here?" he replied.

Frustratingly, *spying on you* were the only words that came to mind. Before I landed on a good lie, he closed the distance between us and—weirdly—hugged me, awkward and wooden but warm bodied. He smelled like trees, like the night smelled.

"I don't sleep much," I finally offered helplessly.

He stepped back. He was one of those guys that, even grown, you could see the little boy in his face . . . or maybe that was because that was the only him I knew. We stared at each other for a beat. I wrapped my arms across and around myself.

"It's good to see you," I said, distant and polite. "Have you been back for a while?"

He shrugged. "I'm going to NYU in the fall. Track scholarship. I'm with my aunty and uncle for the summer." The quirks of his accent came back to me suddenly, the way his consonants squeezed narrow and small between vowels stretched wide, the way he sounded cheerful saying anything at all. He seemed completely unruffled to be caught lurking around our neighborhood at 3:00 a.m.

"That's not . . . what I pictured," I offered. I'd pictured the outback and a farm, maybe some kangaroos in the distance.

I nodded to the equipment in his hands, my natural reserve warring with a curiosity that was by now gnawing my guts. "What's this for?"

"Um, well . . . it's . . ." He finally had the decency to look sheepish and furtive for a moment. He paused a beat, as if connecting one thing to another. "Did you get my letter?"

My skin flared with guilt and I looked into the sky as if the moon was intensely interesting and it was the first time I'd ever seen it. "Yeah," I said. "I'm so busy. I just . . ." I trailed off. "I think you said you wanted to ask me something." I tried to sound like I only vaguely remembered it.

Elias studied me a moment longer, unreadable. "You wanna come over?" He nodded down the street in the direction of his aunt and uncle's house. "I live in the basement now," he added hopefully. "My aunty and uncle watch this show on coin collecting before they go to bed. It's like taking an Ambien. It's easy to sneak in and out."

I'd been in his aunt's bakery a few times over the years. She decorated it with Australian flags and new age crystals and little feminist Etsy cross-stitches, which irked Father James but not enough to keep him away from the cookies. Mrs. Khan baked goods that were some ingenious combination of Bangladeshi and Australian, and she wore T-shirts that said things like Goddess Onboard.

"Umm." I looked behind me. "It's . . . three in the morning. You might be a kidnapper." Thea watched a lot of *Dateline*, and the reenactments on there were things you couldn't unsee. I twirled my purity ring, delicate and etched with a cross, my dad had given me at a special father-daughter church ball in ninth grade. It stood for more or less a promise that I would not go with guys into their basements at 3:00 a.m. and that I'd save my body for marriage.

"I'm not dodgy, mate, I promise."

"That's exactly what an Australian kidnapper would say."

"We don't have kidnappers in Australia," he lied. And

then he nibbled his lip nervously.

Some people are so good-looking that even when they're feeling insecure you don't read it that way. Thea, black haired and beautiful, had those looks, and Elias, I surmised, did too. But he also had the world's worst poker face—which again reminded me of him as a kid. It was this weird sense of being strangers but also familiar. And right now he looked nervous I'd say no.

If the night hadn't stretched out so long ahead of me, if he hadn't looked like he somehow badly needed me to say yes, I wouldn't have gone. But given all that, my curiosity was too much to resist. And so I followed him home.

His room had that slightly dirty yet thrilling smell of boyness: sweat and oceany soap and guy socks. Science fiction books lay scattered on the floor, and his walls were covered in movie posters: a bunch I couldn't read the titles of because they were in a foreign language, and also *Touching the Void*, *Fight Club*, *The Shawshank Redemption*. On his dresser there was a photo of him and his parents on a tropical beach: his dad, pinkish and freckled and bespectacled; his mom, brown skinned and lanky with wavy hair like his. Elias looked like some combination of the two of them: the earnest expression and strong cheekbones of his dad, his skin and hair a lighter echo of his mother's.

He looked unprepared for me and earnest as he tidied up, his Australian good manners almost otherworldly. I twirled my purity ring like a rosary. He watched me as I walked around his room. I kept waiting for him to ask his big question from his letter, but he didn't.

"World of Warcraft." I pointed to a game case lying on the floor. It was something Thea and I had played when we were younger.

He smiled just a touch. "Wanna play?"

I nodded. "Yeah."

We sat and he fired up his console. I'm something of a ringer when it came to World of Warcraft, and I got competitive fast. The game stretched on, and rain pattered on the window; and strangely we fell into an old shape: me quiet and Elias talking, telling me what he'd been doing since that one day I'd known him.

"My uncle and aunty are hosting me until I move into the dorms in late August. I'm studying sports medicine." He paused, his onscreen man died, and he gave a small shiver. "And I need the scholarship. We're broke."

"I thought you lived on a farm."

"We left. Moved to an apartment outside Sydney for Dad's crappy new job."

47

"Why?" I asked, it hitting me in the gut that all these years while I'd pictured him there, he wasn't.

He laid down the controller on his lap for a moment and looked at me.

"He lost the job. Australia is experiencing a cornucopia of delights right now. Wildfires, droughts. It's not an easy time to be a farmer."

"Oh," I said. I studied him. There was a flare of hurt on his face, sadness under his friendly swagger. I wanted to say something but I didn't know what to say.

"It was easier to get a sports scholarship here in the States. You lot are pretty spindly and weak." He smirked and tapped my elbow with his.

Finally the screen froze *"Mar kosom,"* he whispered, and then raised his eyebrows at me. "Sorry, that means something rude in Bengali." No matter how many times he whacked the console, it wouldn't come unstuck.

"You speak Bengali?"

"A little. From my relatives. We go to Bangladeshi weddings sometimes in Sydney. Our extended family's Muslim but we're kinda nonpracticing. My grandma would give me the look of death if she heard me swearing, though."

A long silence stretched between us. It wasn't comfortable, or easy. This faraway boy, he wanted something from me, I just didn't know what.

Looking past my hand where it rested, he gazed at my bare knee. Then he held out his hand to compare. I could see just the tiniest hint of a scar on his palm, and it took my breath away a little. It made me feel like we had some claim to a tiny scar-shaped piece of each other. Which was strange. Because we'd met only once.

"What were *you* doing? Outside at three a.m. looking for me?" he asked.

I hesitated. I picked at imaginary lint, looked out the window to see if the moon still existed.

"I don't sleep, so I walk," I said. "I just happened to see you." I waited for the inevitable unsolicited advice. When you have insomnia, people either say they have trouble sleeping too (like for an hour a night) or look at you like you must be exaggerating. They don't get that you are living in a reality where you'd sell ten years of your life to get through a whole night in unconscious oblivion. If I had a dime for every person who told me to smell lavender before bed, I'd be a rich woman.

But Elias squinted with a kind of cocky grin. He had interesting eyes. Hazel with rust streaks, long full eyelashes.

•

"I can fix that," he said.

"Ha," I said flatly.

"What were *you* doing?" I asked. I wanted to ask why he'd written me, but I also didn't want to know. It was too intimate, too tied to something I didn't like to remember. It felt surrounded by an electric fence.

We sat for a moment quietly. I waited for him to explain himself. And then his eyes trailed to the black and yellow boxes he'd placed on his dresser. There was a long pause. Rain continued to gently patter on the window, almost undetectable except for the silence.

"Looking for something. That's why I wrote to you. I wanted to know if you could help me find it."

"Help you find what?"

He shrugged. "Supernatural activity." He swallowed.

I couldn't tell if he was joking, so I let a long, awkward pause stretch out before I said anything.

"Ghosts?" I finally asked, my voice neutral.

He lowered his chin in a nod.

"On the Christopouloses' roof?"

"On the roof, around cemeteries, in churches. They could be anywhere."

I nodded slowly. Mentally, I was already putting Elias

into a neat and tidy box: the box full of people who believed in ghosts and therefore were not to be taken seriously. I stared at him like he must be joking. He was looking down at his knee but then looked up at me, dead serious.

"*Why?*" I asked.

He looked away. "It was this or collecting stamps."

He was being evasive, I could see. But as someone who's sort of permanently evasive, I didn't want to press.

"Why me?"

He looked disappointed for a moment, then blew a breath and leaned back on his palms on the rug. He tilted his head and squinted at me with a half smile.

"I need someone who knows how to climb trees and make out with them," he said. "It's the only thing I'm missing."

I felt my face turn red. Mentally, I sized up the distance between the girl I was now and the one I was the day Elias knew me: tame in my fuzzy pajamas, risk averse, as far from a Loch Ness Monster as a potato from a cheetah. My inner wild had gone so far underground I barely remembered it.

"Okay, seriously, you're the only person I know here."

He shook his head. "I just . . . wanted to know if you'd like to come with me sometime. Ghost hunting."

I pictured a ghost shot through with an arrow.

"Helping you look for things I know for certain do not exist is not really high on my priority list," I finally said, hiding my cheeks behind my hands.

Elias was undeterred, waiting for an answer.

"I can't sneak out in the middle of the night with a guy. My dad's super strict. It's like the trifecta of wrong things." I held up my purity ring to show him.

"That is severely unintimidating." He shrugged.

A long silence.

"Maybe we'll find things that will amaze and astound you," he said, gesturing like a game show host.

"I do long to be amazed and astounded," I admitted dryly.

"Will you?" The cocky half smile dropped from his face and there was, for a moment, a deeper thing under his irrepressible friendliness. Elias was the kind of guy who seemed as if he wouldn't mind showing his belly to a bear. And he also seemed lonely. His hand was still close to my knee, and he reached out to touch my scar, his finger light as a feather. I pulled my leg away.

"Don't ruin it," I said.

"Oh God, I wasn't making a move on you." He cleared his throat and held up his hand in Scout's honor formation, which apparently was the same in Australia. "I swear. You're not even my type. Seriously, you would literally have to hold a gun to my head to get me to try to make a move." His mouth turned up at one corner.

"That's very flattering. Thank you."

In that moment, I didn't wonder if he was telling me something he thought I needed to hear just so I'd come back. I was relieved. I wanted Elias's friendship, from the start. I didn't live and breathe romance like Thea.

Elias crossed his heart with his finger and smiled. "Seriously, I promise if you hang out with me at night, I will never make a move on you. And I never break a promise. Just put a signal in the window, like something to let me know."

I considered.

"Sometime if I'm up in the night, I'll come with you," I said. I was mostly lying.

"That won't last long because I'm going to fix your sleep."

"Okay, Elias."

"Maybe you'll even sleep better tonight. Because what I'm going to do for you, I've already started doing. It's very subtle."

"Ha," I said, though he looked serious.

He walked me to the door and opened it to the drizzly rain.

"See you around, Cassie."

I nodded. "Okay."

Our conversation still felt unfinished. There was more to Elias's letter than what he said, I knew. And it feels strange to remember it now. How when he came back, I had the upper hand.

I walked home on my tree-lined street, past soaked suburban houses, lawn mowers, swing sets. The rain was now the lightest mist tickling my arms. I tried to turn Elias back to the distant figure I'd envisioned for so long, someone not quite real, but I couldn't.

It turned out he was an optimist: I didn't sleep that night after all. I watched the sun come up the same as I did most mornings, with eyes that wouldn't shut.

I thought he reached out to me because he never really

noticed or cared all those years that I ignored him. But now I understand the opposite is true. He noticed and cared and forgave me anyway. Once Elias got attached to things, he could not let them go.

I guess we came together that night like we were the only two people on an island, which in a way, we were. We were two people on an island on a wild and tumultuous planet. And we were awake. We were two people awake at the same time of night.

It would rain for seventy days.

I would know Elias for seventy-eight.

The world would end in one hundred fifty-four days, or something like that.

I look through the small window in the eave of the tilted wall of the Rose Hotel and comb through all the things we kept hidden from the world.

Chapter 5

"*PEW, PEW, PEW!*" GABE SHOUTED.

The next morning near the crack of dawn, Sister Suzanne and I sat in the parish library, cataloging the books on one of the ancient parish computers. Every time Sister Suzanne went off to do something, I tried to search Elias on my phone, but he had a subnuclear-size social media presence; if you split his online footprint in half, you'd create an atomic bomb. I was feeling like I'd imagined the entire night yet was also concerned Sister Suzanne might have some kind of nun ESP that could stare into my soul and see me in Elias's room.

Gabe and his best friend, Barney, were in the meantime tearing everything up.

"I'm sorry," I said to Sister Suzanne as we watched the boys turn a book of archaic poetry into a gun, then their sleeves into guns, then dust rags into guns. "Thea needed me to take them."

Sister Suzanne, who saw children as both gifts from God and the wild beasts that they were, was pragmatic.

"I'll give you guys a dollar if you can find a four-leaf clover," she suddenly said to the boys, giving me a look. They stopped in their tracks. She shuffled them outside and I could see her through the window, gesturing, showing them where to stay so that they were in our range of sight. They both knelt and began searching the grass.

Then she came back inside, shaking her head. "I'm feeling so validated in my life choices right now."

Being around holy people often made me feel claustrophobic, but being with Sister Suzanne was like drinking from this bright, clear stream. It was like she carried this light with her, and I always wanted to bask in it even though I didn't believe where it came from was real.

"If you like that book on Saint Eia, you should go to that exhibit in the city, *Saints in the Dark*. Supposedly they have her famous golden stone at the New York Public Library . . . Bryant Park branch, the one with the stone lions." She leaned emphatically closer. "Act your age, sneak off and see it."

"I don't think that's what people my age do when they sneak out," I said. Also you'd have to pay me a million dollars to take a train through a tunnel under a river like some fearless explorer. I wasn't Ferdinand Magellan.

"How would I know? I'm a nun."

This was a thing with us: Sister Suzanne trying to get me out of my shell, giving me suggestions that were completely off the mark about how I should act more seventeenish. I felt, but couldn't prove, that she had been fairly wild in her day. I also knew she had a deep, lust-fueled crush on Bruce Springsteen, which she confessed to me once after having an extra glass of sherry at bingo.

I was more intrigued than I let on, though. I hadn't thought for one minute the stone was real. The reality of Saint Eia was muddled, and I wasn't sure where the truth ended and myth began. The *Celts* were real. *Saint* Eia was real, but I'd assumed the golden stone wasn't. Definitely the floating on a *leaf* wasn't. Unfortunately, my dad never let us go into the city, though Thea snuck in from time to time.

Out on the lawn, just beyond the boys and their futile clover hunt, we saw Father James pull up in his car and cross the lawn toward the priests' residence. He looked more than usually grouchy.

"He's mad," she said, giving me that look of someone who's about to tell you something juicy. "So I was getting our groceries at ShopRite. It was one of those group trips where we all descend on the store in the van like *March of the Penguins*." She nodded out the window. "He was there talking to the cashier about some magazine he thought was too trashy for them to display, always with the boobs. You know, just some really solid monologuing."

"I'm familiar with the monologuing. Go on."

"Well, that kid from New Zealand, Ellish . . ."

I felt myself going still as a deer in headlights. You couldn't buy grapes in Green Valley without everyone hearing about it, so of course it was inevitable that people would know about Elias. And it was Sister Suzanne, so of course she got everything around 25 percent wrong.

"I guess Ellish must have overheard Father James, because he came walking up in the middle of the whole thing with this basket of potato chips and an absurdly large pile of *Bustees*." *Bustees* being a magazine full of naked women who were exclusively DD or above. (On a side note, when people think of nuns, they assume they're prim and out of the loop and that they would never know what *Bustees* is. This is not true.)

"He stands right behind Father James," she went on, her eyes out the window on Father James, "and just started loading like ten issues of *Bustees* onto the conveyor belt. I think he did it just to make him mad, I mean, it was more issues of *Bustees* than any one person could really need." She glanced at me to make sure I was following along, which I was. And then she laughed into her hand. "Father James looked back to him, gaping. Ellish just smiles and nods at Father James as politely as can be and says, 'Go big or go home, am I right?' I think Father James nearly swallowed his tongue. Personally, I was dead. I died."

I stared out the window, away from her. It didn't surprise me that Elias had done it. Even just knowing him for one day and one night in my entire life, it seemed like something he'd do for a laugh. But getting on Father James's bad side meant more these days than it had used to. In the spring he'd used his newfound sway to get a kid expelled for drawing devil horns on the portrait of Sister Ann in the main school hall, and he'd talked half the parish into believing Bishop O'Ryan was a bit of a heretic because he didn't think we needed to convert Presbyterians. He was that perfect combination of insecure and vindictive, which as far as I could tell is the recipe for every guy who ever unleashed the calamities of history. I didn't like to think of him noticing Elias at all.

Father James disappeared inside, while in the foreground, Gabe and Barney had abandoned the search for clovers and were now stumbling around in their raincoats trying to pull each other to the ground. I knew how this would go: inevitably one of them would whack the other hard into a rock or something, there would be tears, and then they'd recover and do it all again.

"Little stinkers," Sister Suzanne said, with something between affection and horror. Gabe was eating a booger while Barney was trying to kick him in the butt. Gabe's shoe was already wet from being dropped into the parish toilet earlier in the day. I loved that kid more than I loved myself, but watching him and Barney just live their lives seemed to be a pretty good indicator of why a world dominated by men might be more than a little in the shitter.

"Don't you think the Bible sounds suspiciously like it was written for dudes by dudes?" I said to Sister Suzanne, knowing she'd follow my train of thought. I was always trying to stir the pot to see if I could rattle her, but I never could.

She was wiping down some high shelves on her tiptoes so she spoke over her shoulder. "It's not the dudes I'm in it for, it's the grace. And you're saying this to a woman who's not allowed to give sermons but has to listen to Father James talk about how there's a chicken out there with two butts and only one head."

"I thought Thea made that up."

She leveled a gaze at me that said Thea did not make it up.

"Uh-oh," she added under her breath. Father James had reemerged from the residence and was crossing the grass toward us. Most likely to ask her about something.

"Hold that thought; I need a cigarette," she said. And she disappeared out the door and down the hall.

She didn't come back.

Just like that, she Father Jamesed me.

That afternoon, Thea and I tried to catch the sun between the heavy gray clouds, lying on the loungers and reading *People*, both of us being reliant on celebrity gossip like oxygen. I was still troubled for Elias after what Sister Suzanne had told me, a worry buried so deep I couldn't put my finger on it.

Dad was working in the garden, which had gone to seed when my mom had left. I remember watching her go, pulling out of our driveway in her blue Hyundai Elantra. I suppose some moms fantasize about riding away from their responsibilities and never looking back, but my mom had actually done it when Gabe was only three months old.

She'd been a distant blur of a person even when she was around: always distracted, always sad. She'd never been the person we'd gone to with injuries or accomplishments or homework. She had told us, when she left, that she'd be visiting soon, but she never did.

Now, beside the deck, my dad turned over a large rotted log, revealing a cluster of baby snakes. Exposed to the light, they curled and twirled wildly and slithered away into the grass.

"They're off to protest the Skyline View," I quipped. "I wonder where their little signs are." But the joke went over in silence. My dad only sat back on his heels, dropping the moldy leaves into a compost bucket as we watched the pale snakes squiggle away.

"Father James takes it too far," he said, "but he's saying what a lot of people are thinking. People are tired of the disrespect." He shook his head. "That stunt with the Virgin Mary . . . I'm glad he dealt with it."

I'd seen how it hurt my dad to see things he found sacred insulted. It wasn't that I didn't know pain was the reason people listened to Father James in the first place. But it made a small twisting feeling of surprise in my chest, the resigned way he said it . . . or maybe that he said it at all.

"He means well," he added.

"He called people *snakes*, Dad."

"Other people say worse about Catholics," Thea chimed in. "He's standing up for us." I leaned back in the lounger, feeling slightly untethered. Apparently, Thea and my dad had had a secret meeting where they'd decided Father James wasn't a jackass.

My dad laid his shovel against the log and dug out some rocks with his hand. "Anyway, he doesn't mean half of what he says. Nobody's perfect, Cass."

I wanted to point out you could also say nobody's perfect about Charles Manson or Ted Bundy . . . but Dad had crossed the lawn to go get his weed whacker. And anyway, I trod lightly with my family. It was a dance, this kind of hiding, a slippery slope of showing them who I was that I didn't want them to see. I was faithless, after all.

And according to Father James, that meant I was prone to all sorts of resentment. Why else would you be mad at a priest who told everyone greenhouse gases were just propaganda invented by China?

I swatted away some mosquitoes and finally walked inside and upstairs, flopping onto my bed. I went on looking at but not really reading my *People*—even though it was the kind of article I lived for, about how celebrities look when they're grocery shopping.

On the wall by my headboard was a greeting card my dad had taped there: a picture of a beach inscribed with this poem about how Jesus and a guy walk along a beach, leaving two pairs of footprints behind them. But whenever times get hard, Jesus's footprints disappear. When the guy asks why Jesus disappears during the bad times, Jesus basically is like *no, dummy, there's only one set of footprints because that's when I was carrying you.*

My dad loved that story; Jesus had saved him once, he sometimes said, though he didn't say from what (my dad was a private kind of guy). His belief carried him, and I envied that, but we saw different things when we looked at the same blue sky and there was no way for us to change our retinas.

My dad existed in a world where I still believed and was

saved, and everything was looked after by God, and Father James was only a brash man who said unkind things that amounted to nothing. My world had icebergs crumbling with worse to come, and men like Father James lighting the matches.

Finally, I sat up, looking around my room, my cautiousness evaporated. Eyeing my collection of horse figurines, I picked one up—the biggest one, black with a white star on her forehead—and placed it in my window where I thought Elias would see it. And then I sensed someone watching me.

I looked to see Gabe standing in the hall, naked from the waist down. He hadn't yet learned to be embarrassed about anything.

"Come sit with me while I poop," he said casually, and then shuffled inside, bare-assed and oblivious.

And, because I loved him beyond what was humanly reasonable, I went.

Chapter 6

TO REALLY PICTURE THE DARK AGES, YOU have to imagine the world from the sky; imagine you're a bird or a cloud or the moon looking down on the earth in AD 499. Rome, having rotted from the inside for years, has fallen to invaders, and with it a light has gone out in Europe. There's a big shadowy hole where Roman order used to be: the wide Roman roads crisscrossing the European continent have fallen into disrepair and gone overgrown. Branching out around the capital city like scattered stars are the fires of warring tribes: Saxons, Goths, Visigoths, Ostrogoths, Huns. It's a continent scarred by violence and uncertainty, each night illuminated only by tiny fires, pushing back against the world-devouring dark. You have to try to picture it from the sky downward to see how terrifying and beautiful it is, the glittering black nights and the golden-fired seeds of a future no one can see coming.

This was the wild and dangerous world that Saint Eia traversed when she left her home in the green woods among the Celts to chase down her precious stone and murder the people who stole it from her.

There she was when she started out, completely sure the world was full of magic and faeries, only to find that in the outside world everybody saw something different in the universe around them. The Saxons saw dragons and thunder gods and charms that brought luck to the people who held them. The Huns saw prophecy and water spirits and the moon. The Gauls saw their ancestors watching over them in the form of gods.

Eia learned this through snatches of language she could glean along the way, but there was so much lost in the spaces in between one person talking to another. It must have been a shock for her, to find out that the world she knew was only one of many ideas of what the world was.

It was on her way through Lutetia, now Paris, where,

according to *Saint Eia of the Celts*, she heard a growing story about a humble man who claimed to be the son of God. The story had wings on its feet, crossing the world faster than she could dream.

And though it gets fuzzy here on how it all went down, she turned away from her warrior goddesses and chose to be baptized by men. I wondered, though it was sacrilegious to ask, had she ever wished to take it back?

And I needed to know, did she ever find her lost relic? To go all that way, to brave the violence of a wild continent, she must have valued it more than life.

That night, I read with Gabe's small frame curled beside me in the bed, losing myself in the past. Occasionally I'd gaze around at my dimly lit room, at the clock, at everything I'd arranged so perfectly on my shelves. For a while, I drifted off to sleep.

By the time a sound roused me, I'd forgotten what I'd been waiting for. I looked to my window, trying to make sense of it: some animal trying to get in, but how could it climb so high . . . ?

I slipped away from Gabe's warmth and looked outside to see Elias was on the lawn, a rock hefted high in his hand about to be launched. He didn't say a word, just dropped the rock mid-heft and nodded his chin up toward me in greeting.

I glanced back at Gabe, who was either fast asleep or pretending well. It wasn't out of the question for him to follow me places after pretending to be asleep like this. But his steady breathing told me he wasn't faking. I tiptoed out.

Outside on the lawn it was hot, and lightning bugs were weaving through the rain.

Elias's bedhead was epic.

"I thought you were a possum," I said.

"That's sadly indicative of how many times someone's come to sneak you out." He moved close to me; I stepped back. "You coming ghost hunting?" he asked, trying to push his hair in one direction though it kept bouncing back to make a point. Its thick curliness was rather glorious. He scrunched down his eyebrows unsurely, as if he was nervous I'd say no.

"Yeah, I'm coming," I said.

Naturally, Elias thought we should start at the cemetery.

He handed me a flashlight, a tiny black box, a wrist strap with something gadgety attached to the front, and a plastic container that looked like a small toolbox. "One's an infrared sensor," he finally said, "the other's a laser grid. Here's your wrist recorder, it's high-quality audio, definitely suggest you keep it recording the whole time. It'll pick up things you don't notice. Here's your ghost box . . ." His drawn-out vowels made all these words sound prettier than they were.

"For the ectoplasm," I said flatly, kidding, but Elias shook his head earnestly.

"Ectoplasm's rubbish, mate."

I blinked at him, amused at that level where you can't laugh but your chest feels like it's full of bubbles because the funny goes deeper than laughing. He was unbearably nerdy and I couldn't tell whether I wanted to hug him or squirm or both.

"Just so you know, this is . . . not rational," I said.

Cast in the halo of my flashlight, Elias pressed his lips firmly together, tightening the strap around my wrist and not looking at me. "Is that your official statement?" he said, with bone-deep confidence. "I'm glad you got it out of the way. That must be a relief."

"Did it cost a lot?" I asked.

His long lashes fluttered a bit. "Only all my savings." Which deepened the mystery of it.

———✳———

We stumbled around among the headstones in our rain-coats. I occupied myself by waving my electromagnetic frequency detector absurdly with one hand while using my flashlight to illuminate gravestones with the other. The wealthiest dead people were still lording it over everyone else with big obelisks and crypts, which was typical. The rain fell on all the gravestones and splattered up at my face. Every so often I'd look up at Elias and he'd be watching me nervously, his mouth open like he was about to say something. And he seemed to be kind of . . . steering our path, but trying to do it subtly, which he was not very good at (being subtle, and steering).

Finally, when the rain really started coming down hard, he tugged on my wrist and pulled me toward a stone structure that turned out to be a mausoleum. We ducked inside and out of the rain.

"Just till it lets up," he said, looking around.

I nodded, studying the inscription at the back of the tomb.

VAN DOREN
AD MELIORA

I stood there wondering why the name sounded familiar to me and what the inscription meant.

"Toward better things," Elias said behind me.

I turned to give him an impressed look, but as I did, he held up his phone to show me he'd looked it up. Then he sank down to sit with his back against a stone wall, folding his lanky legs to fit. I sank down a couple of feet away; every time he scooted closer for warmth, I scooted back. (Thea liked to tease me about how I treated all guys like they had typhoid.) He had huge feet.

"This is better things?" I said, looking around.

"I think they mean the afterlife, you philistine." Elias diligently scanned the enclosed darkness with his tools, biting his lip in concentration, his hazel eyes serious and focused. But after a while, he gave up, sank back, and watched the rain.

Finally, he thrust out a hand, thumb extended upward, and raised his eyebrows at me.

We played thumb war several times. I kept beating him.

"You're impossible to find online," I said.

"Waste of time. And so are you, by the way." He looked up. "Impossible to find, that is, not a waste of time." I was surprised that he'd looked for me.

"I heard about the ShopRite," I said. "And the *Bustees*."

Elias jerked his eyes up to mine and a mischievous yet sheepish smile spread across his face.

"It's not a great idea to mess with that guy. You don't want to get on his bad side." I tried to sound more casual than I felt.

Elias smirked at me, cocky. "I can't help it if I love the curvy ladies as much as they love me."

I leaned back against a wall. "My hypothesis is that they do not love you, on account of you being a ghost hunter with a room full of sci-fi posters. My hypothesis is you were being a smart-ass."

Elias shrugged, brushed something off his sleeve.

"Father James thinks anyone he has personal beef with is going to hell," I said. "It's like God is this mobster who owes him a favor. He can get you in trouble. Just be careful."

"I don't go to Mary Immaculate, and that guy's an ass-hole." He looked at me and shrugged, amused and also a bit frayed, the heavier thing and the lighter thing mixed together.

He studied me for a while, and at the awkward phys-ical distance I kept between our feet. I felt the prickling of something coming that I did not want to hear. He was gearing up to say it; I just couldn't imagine what it might be.

"I wasn't honest, about my letter. Why I wrote you. Why *you*. It's not the making out with trees."

I stared at him and waited.

He sank back, reluctant. He ran his hands along the cold, damp stone floor, thinking.

"It's not just a random hobby. I'm looking for ghosts because I just . . . saw them," he said, looking up and out at the rain.

I followed his eyes and wondered if by "just" he meant right now, like if he was trying to do one of those ghost stories where it turns out *the ghost is right behind you!!*

But he was too serious, sincere. He looked at me and smoothed a wayward strand of bangs out of his eye.

"When?" I asked.

He stared at me up from under his eyebrows. "When do you think?"

I blinked at him for several seconds, confused. And then *I got it*. Chills swam over me. Shivering, I felt the hot anxiety of that day, the thing we'd seen but told no one about. The sound of metal. The train in the lake.

Do you see them? I remembered him asking me. All this time, I'd thought he meant survivors.

"They were circles of light, rising from the water," he said now. "One for every person on the train who died, I think." He was quiet for a moment. "I always wanted to ask if you saw them too. But the other night . . . when we talked . . ." He shrugged. "Obviously not."

I shook my head. I chose my words carefully.

"Elias, you didn't see them either. Not really."

Elias ran his hand along a seam on his leg, his eyelids heavy over his eyes, not looking at me.

"How do you know that?" he asked gently.

"Because I was there." I ducked my head, trying to catch his eyes. "We can't get our heads around ending, so we make up ghosts."

Long silence.

"People see ghosts and things all the time," he said. "*Normal* people. There are people who could tell you exactly who was in the room after they technically flatlined and then came back, people who've survived plane crashes and they've seen the spirits of the people around them leave their bodies. My grandma has this friend in Bangladesh who works as a psychic for the Dhaka Metropolitan Police; he literally solves *crimes* by talking to ghosts." He tilted his head, smiling. "How do you explain that?"

"How do I explain ghost detectives?" I said. "Weirdly, I haven't thought about it." He looked at me from under his eyebrows.

I knew he wanted sincerity from me, but I was there that day. I saw it too. And I had seen the opposite: a full stop, an empty place, unfixable loss. How could we have seen the same thing and come away with something so different? Mine being the loss of magic, his being the beginning of it.

We sat quietly for a long time.

"I mean, I'll probably never find anything. I get that."

"I'm sorry I can't be your proof," I finally said.

Elias shifted, and we were quiet for a few more moments. I thought he was annoyed with me and ready to go home, rain be damned. But instead, he took off his rain jacket, pulled off the sweatshirt he was wearing over a T-shirt, put his rain jacket back on, and balled the shirt up and laid it on the floor. He was, if anything, unfazed.

"Okay, the first thing I'm going to do to help you sleep is hypnotize you. I heard how to do it on a podcast."

"It won't work," I said. "Especially not here."

"It will. We've got all night."

"You have delusions of grandeur."

"Thank you."

"It's not a compliment."

He patted the balled-up sweatshirt.

I sighed, giving in.

I lay down.

"Okay, listen. You're on this beach," he said. "Palm trees. White sand. Blue water. It's so safe."

I could hear Elias shift back against the stone wall as he talked about the imaginary beach. I had to admit, he painted a good picture. I felt relaxed, though no closer to dropping off.

After a while, he stopped talking.

I sat up and squinted at him in the dark.

He was asleep.

I watched him, annoyed, as I was rightfully annoyed with anyone who could fall asleep easily *anywhere*, much less in mausoleums. Looking at the scar on his open palm made me rub my hand along my knee.

Studying him, I had time to realize I was scared of him. Spending time with him was like opening a window to get air. I didn't know why he chose me to share his blood with when we were kids. And I supposed that's what happens when someone who awes you also chooses to be interested in you. You can't help but fear it, and you don't want to let it disappear, and you want to be enough to deserve it. I guessed that was a story as old as time.

We walked toward home past the Rose Hotel that night. It was faded and glorious, with beaux arts angels on the parapets and insurmountable obstacles keeping us out: a gated bridge across the river, an electrified fence, another barbed wire fence closer to the building itself. It had been built in the 1920s, and when they'd been alive, the owners had kept its old-world charm . . . either to be distinctive or because they couldn't afford updates, or probably both.

It was all sagging a bit now, and the whole building seemed to list a little to the left. The hotel's inheritance had been mired in controversy ever since the owners died on the train. The management had tried to make a go of keeping it open, but it had been shut down soon after, and stayed that way. Supposedly, the problem was that the cliffs were eroding underneath it, and the foundations would take millions to fix and nobody wanted to pay. So year after year, the hotel had gotten more overgrown and disheveled.

And suddenly, it landed on me: the reason I knew the

name we'd seen in the cemetery. How Elias had steered me to that grave on purpose.

It was the Van Doren family who'd owned the Rose Hotel.

"They're the ghosts you're looking for," I said, annoyed. Elias liked my annoyance. He grinned crookedly.

"If they're anywhere, they're in there. I just haven't figured out how to get in yet," he said. "Everything else is a warm-up to that."

"No," I said, to all of it, everything.

He fluttered his eyelashes at me.

"We could get arrested. There could be snakes."

"Why snakes?"

I shrugged. "It's just a thing that could happen. Also, I'm not ten. I'm not, like . . . the Boxcar Children."

Elias shrugged in his casually undeterred way.

I got to my house about an hour before dawn. We didn't see any ghosts that night, nor would we any night. We'd never find the spirits Elias so badly wanted to find. His hunt for the dead was a fool's errand; I knew that from the start.

But it was too late for me. As much as I was good at keeping my distance from the world at large in all its unforeseeable dangers, I couldn't help but let Elias in. And so that's how you end up looking for ghosts even when you don't believe in them or much of anything at all.

Elias had tied me close to him when we were kids, through a thin line of blood. He had slipped under my defenses long before I had them.

Chapter 7

WE DIDN'T MEAN, AT FIRST, TO HAVE A secret friendship: it just kind of happened by way of being nocturnal. It was the timing that was secret, and the friendship that followed.

Every night that I assumed he wasn't coming because it was too late or raining too hard, he showed up with his bedhead and his grin and his armfuls of equipment. And so we spent the next four weeks hunting Green Valley's nonexistent ghosts: in mausoleums, in graveyards, near houses where we knew people had recently died. That's how mercenary we were.

While the Van Dorens were Elias's *ghosts of choice*, we

didn't have that many options as far as the family went: just the cemetery where they were buried and the impenetrable hotel. We'd walk by it in our travels, Elias scanning the grounds as if he was casing the joint, but we'd push on, twistedly, to other places, like nursing homes and the hospital.

In the daytime, things were different. We led separate lives. I saw him twice during those early weeks, but he didn't see me. Once, he was sprinting on the Mary Immaculate track; I was driving past. I thought it couldn't be him. All traces of the easygoing boy I knew, the one constantly relaxed and amused, was gone. Running, he was all focus: legs pumping, body muscled in a way I hadn't noticed, his face intent and serious.

The other time, driving by the Grotto, as we called it (a small inlet that leaked off the edge of the reservoir), I saw him diving off a rock, doing a backflip and landing in deep water where four other people were lounging on rocks looking like gods. He was surrounded by friends, which he accumulated quickly. I knew this mostly through Thea, who kept track of people, and especially hot ones.

In any case, no one would have dreamed we were spending our nights together: golden, center-of-the-world

Elias, and me with my convent-adjacent life. And it intrigued me all the more that in spite of his growing roster of admirers, every night he came looking for me.

We settled into each other like two people related by blood, even if that blood had gotten mushed together in an unofficial kind of way. We talked about crushes. (He had a thing for a couple of Bengali celebrities I hadn't heard of, and I liked Indiana Jones–era Harrison Ford.) He talked about how much he resented the phrases "one hundred and ten percent" and "it is what it is," while I filled him in on my general impressions of the parish ladies (mostly polite bordering on ruthless) and told him about the dance our church had when the dads gave us our purity rings. ("That's bizarre," he said. "Americans are weird.")

I discovered, with Elias, that I could actually be rather dazzling. There was something glittering about the way we could talk, like I could say the most obscure and lopsided thought in my head, and he would get it.

I grew a fast love for sci-fi movies and Lord of the Rings. I worried about his eyesight as he scrolled through his phone in the dark, looking up ghost stories. He was genuinely interested in Saint Eia and her golden stone, especially her stone being at the New York Public Library as if it were a real thing, and he didn't laugh that I was a nonbeliever of anything who also wanted to be a nun.

Elias *got* me, and I got him, as if we'd known each other since birth. But every night, lying awake, I twirled my ring and went over these things in my mind, how he rubbed his palm scar raw when he became thoughtful, the way being around him was as simple as breathing.

Still, there were nights he couldn't get out or needed to catch up on sleep, and those were the nights I escaped into the dusty goneness of the Dark Ages. I read how Saint Eia finally arrived within the city limits of a crumbled Rome after months of weary wandering in which she nearly lost her life to violence, and starvation, and plague. And how she found her golden stone had been sold to an obscure tribe of seafaring Vandals, and therefore had passed beyond tracking.

This is where the trail went cold. Baptized or not, she killed about six Saxons in cold blood, but it didn't get the sacred object back and it didn't bring her the satisfaction she'd hoped. With no leads except that the tribe lived along the shores of Carthage, with little hope of finding them, she set off for the sea.

—✳—

On the news, there was bad weather in faraway places, and the world seemed more chaotic than normal. The awareness of that settled around Green Valley like a cold day when you're bundled up inside. As for us, we had only rain.

Maybe it was the weather wearing on him too, but the following Sunday, Father James's sermon was particularly fiery. The Skyline View controversy had escalated: someone had chained themselves to a pine tree and held up construction for three days. While Thea thought this was hilarious, Father James was not amused.

The protester was an environmentalist from Trace County. She probably shopped at Whole Foods (which along with 666 was basically the mark of the beast). And so, of course, since you had to agree with a group of people on either *everything* or nothing, the woman's fears about the Skyline View must be unfounded. Which to me seemed like ignoring someone who was screaming that you were about to get hit by a bus because they were wearing an ugly sweater.

But half of the Rotary club was so riled up they decided to boycott all Trace County shops. And it started to seem to me that, if anyone was going to welcome the prince of darkness with open arms when Armageddon arrived, it was the sweet ladies of the parish luncheon committee who said God was just working through Father James in mysterious ways.

Plenty of people were leaving our church, migrating over to Our Lady of Sorrows because they were sick of Father James's crap, but I stopped probing Thea and my dad for what the breaking point for them might be. They were both annoyed by Father James and also insistent that he was the best we could hope for when other people were so messed up . . . so *against* us. In other words, there would *be* no breaking point. I fantasized about shouting, throwing myself in the church aisle to kick and scream.

And then, somebody did what I only fantasized about.

The stories piled up over the next couple of weeks. Somebody repurposed the Let It Snow/Le Tits Now letters, stealing them from the shed where they'd been locked away to spell LONE TWIT in front of Father James's residence, the leftover *S* just lying in the grass. The following Sunday, someone took out a classified ad in the local paper that said: *Supreme Deity in search of pastor's help in judging the saved from the damned. Need someone with a keen eye for sin as I am extremely busy and cannot do this kind of thing myself. HELP.*

The next week, Sister Suzanne said, almost hyperventilating from laughter, someone switched the ID card that hung from Father James's rearview mirror with a photo of a Chihuahua in a lobster costume and slapped a bumper sticker next to his license plate that said I'm One Bad Relationship Away from Having 30 Cats.

When I asked Elias about it, we were standing in the darkness outside the house of an elderly woman who'd died a week before, according to the local obituaries. I figured there was a fifty-fifty chance he'd been the one doing all the pranks.

He ignored the question, distracted. "If she's not here," he said, biting his lip and scanning the trees thoughtfully, "she'd be hovering around her loved ones. Does the paper say if she had any relatives?"

"I'm not stalking a dead lady's bereaved relatives," I said.

Elias looked at me as if I was nothing but boundaries.

"Well, let's go to the bridge, then," he said impatiently. The trestle bridge hadn't come up before now, but it had been on my mind, and I guessed it had been on Elias's too. He said the words lightly, but his face had gone serious and heavy. It had always been inevitable, I suppose, that we'd end up where the train had gone under.

We walked to the edge of the river and trailed along it until the reservoir opened out before us. And here we came to the edge of the tracks, where the metal had buckled. There was hardly any sign of it now, no marker or memorial to commemorate what had happened here. But if you looked closely you could see where the metal had been replaced, where the new tracks and bolts weren't as faded as the concrete that held them.

We stood and stared down at the water for a moment, before Elias pulled out his equipment silently. I did the same. We scanned the air for rogue frequencies. Around us, crickets and tree frogs chirped at a deafening volume and rain pattered the leaves. New Jersey sounded like the rain forest.

I felt young and alive above such a watery grave, and also nervous. It took me until later to figure out why.

"Did you do it?" I asked. "The pranks?" But Elias only held up his EMF meter and walked along the bank, either being mysterious or truly uninterested.

"Elias."

Finally he looked up, squinting at me.

"I don't know how you've lived this long without punching that guy in the face," he said.

I studied my hands wrapped around my EMF meter. "I prefer poisoning myself with repressed rage," I said.

"I see that," he said. Not *un*judgmentally.

"People do anger in such a shitty way," I said, to defend myself, "it's like they break more than they fix. I don't wanna break things."

"Getting everything perfect makes you feel safe," he said. "I get it." He stared out at the water, and I felt my skin crawl, like Elias could see right through me. "You were angry when you were little, though," he said. "It was great."

I thought how the young me, so wild and pissed off and hurt, had never seemed that great to me. "I don't know why you wrote me all those years."

He was quiet, like he didn't want to say.

"Will you go home a lot, to visit?" I asked, casting about for anything to change the subject. "Once school starts?"

"Nah. My family saved up forever to buy my fare here, as it is." He kept scanning the water, but just to have something to do with his hands. He scratched at his hair again, like he was itching to get out of his skin. "My parents were elated when I got this scholarship. It was like a life preserver. But I don't wanna do sports medicine, really. I *am* looking forward to seeing snow; I never have."

He looked up at me, like he was embarrassed, and swallowed.

"The beach I was telling you about when I solved your sleep problem—"

"You didn't solve it."

"It's a real place," he went on. "My dad had a job on a pearl farm near Broome when I was a kid. Like, gathering oysters for pearls. And we took a trip there once. It's seriously the most perfect place I've ever seen. In the west of Australia. Very isolated. Don't ask me where, because my mom says it's our secret beach so I can't tell you."

I rolled my eyes. It sounded like a movie.

"But, you know, it's one of those beaches that are going like . . ." And he held up his hand, thumb down. "What with the earth devouring itself and whatnot. The dunes are eroding into the sea." He fiddled with the buttons on his equipment, but I could see the seriousness of his face. "These amazing seabirds live there, but now they're exposed to the wind, which is trashing their nests.

"If I ever go back home, like, for good, I'm gonna call some of those people from One World and get them to help me protect that beach. Like, I'll just annoy them until they sponsor me. Then we'll help reconstruct the dunes. Plant grasses so they don't slip away. Help push back against the water."

He looked at me, cocky and expectant, like he was waiting for me to confirm his genius. I blinked at him.

"What?" he asked.

"You can't fight the ocean," I said, "it's futile. Like . . . it's the *ocean* and you're . . . *a guy*."

He ignored me but smirked.

"Mark my words. If you do this, someone will build a Sandals resort there," I said.

"You're funny," he said flatly, but with pleasure in his eyes. "I wouldn't mind if you came," he said.

"How can I come if you don't tell me where it is?" I was teasing; I knew I wouldn't be caught dead on a plane, much less putting a world between me and Gabe.

I thought he'd tell me then; I figured he was joking. But he only smiled and kept his secret beach to himself.

After about an hour of us standing over the lake like fools, looking for spirits in their watery graves, the sky really opened up, and Elias put his arm over my head as if he could block the rain, and we headed for home. We left the reservoir and the secrets of its dead behind us.

As for the pranks, Elias never admitted it, but the escapades continued anyway. Someone signed up Father James for a dating site for farmers . . . filled the parking lot of the priests' residence with a labyrinth of official-looking orange construction cones (which Father James navigated for two days before realizing it was a joke) . . . created a social media page called "Things Jeff Bezos doesn't want you to know" with fictional "facts" like how every gigabyte makes your phone heavier, just so Father James would repost them when he got tagged.

I knew it was him. What I didn't know, at first, was why he did it . . . why Elias hated Father James with a passion that I'd only seen him reserve for "it is what it is." I only suspected, as much as anything else, it was boredom that led him to it; the same pent-up feeling that *I* had of being somewhere that didn't quite have enough room for me . . . like trying to stretch my arms inside a box. But it was more than that. And I could see it pretty easily even then: that Elias couldn't back down from a fight, even if he wanted to.

Chapter 8

HALFWAY THROUGH THE FIRST WEEK OF
July, to everyone's surprise, the skies cleared and we were
given a week of blue expanses, sun, and air that smelled
like it had been washed clean. The low gray haze of sky
evaporated into a blue sweep dotted by puffy white clouds,
and the grass everywhere turned as green as Ireland.

The sunshine was such a novelty that people swarmed
outside in droves. Kids rode bikes up and down our street;
people walked past our house on their way downtown to
the farmer's market; the Christopouloses started throwing
Frisbees around in their yard. All together, it made Green

Valley look like a Norman Rockwell painting had vomited on a Hallmark movie.

The first nice day Thea, Gabe, and I planted ourselves on towels on the grass that surrounded the Grotto. A waterfall rushed down from the mountain at the water's edge, and the lawn lifted up on all sides like a soft green bowl, making it a heavenly spot for Green Valley's residents to loll around, sunbathe, eat, and talk.

We were lying on our backs on the grass, and Thea was trying to take selfies of us, between talking to people we knew who kept drifting over. They were mostly from Mary Immaculate's youth group, which revolved less around anything holy than it did around water-skiing trips, campouts, and hookups.

"Cass, make your face more like your real human face," Thea said, swiping her dark hair out of her eyes and scrolling back to browse the selfies we'd done so far, and then re-posing. "You look like Gollum."

Thea could say things like this. And I knew she was right: when people took photos of me, my face somehow turned inward like a vampire cowering from sunlight. I knew how people saw us: Thea was the *wow* sister and I was the witty, quiet one.

I didn't really care. Some people fell all over themselves because of Thea's looks, and other people tried to take her down because of it; and it was fairly obvious to me that being female meant you were generally going to be given shit for your looks either way. Though occasionally it happened that somebody would be chatting up Thea and then look over and notice me, and then, like, *really* notice me . . . as if I were a painting you couldn't really see until you were close up.

Finally, with each photo growing increasingly Gollum-like, Thea gave up.

I rolled onto my stomach and showed Gabe how to make a whistle out of a blade of grass, and we whistled at each other quietly—a party of two.

Gabe knew more people at the park than Thea and me combined. After my mom left, practically the whole Mary Immaculate congregation had shown up to babysit for him and bring us casseroles. He was one of those kids who was everybody's kid, spending his summers wandering from house to house in our neighborhood, receiving an endless supply of freezie pops and ice cream and making himself at home in people's living rooms to watch TV.

We rolled onto our backs and looked for the same things in the clouds. All of Gabe's were sweet: "There's a rabbit kissing her baby; there's a Ferris wheel; there's a lady smiling at us." I was trying to see the smile, see the world the way Gabe saw it, and sleepy enough that I almost could; being overtired put my imagination into overdrive. Then Thea pinched me.

Elias had come to stand above us. Thea was adjusting her bikini top.

"Elias, this is my sister, Cassie," she said.

I looked up at him.

"Hey," I said, raising my eyebrows as if to get him to leave.

Elias beamed. "Nice to meet you." With the ease and entitlement of a Victorian picnicker, he plopped down on the other side of Gabe, near my feet, and yanked a piece of grass out of the ground between my toes to make his own grass whistle.

I rolled over and dug my Saint Eia book out of my bag, opening to a random page. I could feel Thea look apologetically at Elias like it was typical for me to be antisocial.

But Elias didn't seem bothered. Within minutes he was teaching Gabe how to make fart noises with his palms, making him giggle uncontrollably, and then how to do a headstand. Thea was sitting up, watching them and laughing, flirting. She liked him, I could tell. Finally, he

and Gabe lay on their backs, exhausted from their headstands, instant best friends. Maybe Elias was *instant best
friends* with everyone, and it wasn't just me. Maybe he
made everyone feel like they were rather dazzling.

"Wanna come swim?" he asked us.

"Cassie doesn't swim," Thea said, assuming he was
addressing *her* mostly. "Our mom said she'd take us but
she never did. I taught myself anyway." She was trying to
portray herself as the brave one, which wasn't hard.

Off they went, Thea barreling into the cold water at
the foot of the falls like a gazelle, Elias right behind her
but more gentle, one hand in Gabe's and the other holding
his nose so that Gabe wouldn't feel embarrassed holding
his too.

As Elias went, he turned to look at me and flashed
me his palm, pointing to his scar, before slipping into the
water. Like he wanted me to know we were connected
even when we pretended not to be.

"I think he likes me," said Thea. The sun was setting and
the clouds were moving in, and we were the last ones
left on the lawn, sunbaked and pleasantly tired and pack-
ing up our things. Elias had trailed off to track practice

around four o'clock, never coming to say goodbye.

I felt myself flush at Thea's words. I supposed I felt possessive. Gabe, meanwhile, was smitten. He kept asking if Elias could be his babysitter and accusing Thea of wanting to keep Elias to herself.

"I've heard he's the one messing with Father James, though," Thea added. She looked thoughtful, a bit conflicted.

"Father James needs to be messed with." I sighed.

She looked unsure. "It's pretty disrespectful. The guy went to seminary. God put him there for a reason."

"You can't technically disrespect someone who tells people solar power gives everyone cancer. It's like saying you're disrespecting a clown."

"Oh, like the people who tie themselves to trees are so great."

I blinked at her, at the quickness with which she batted away anyone calling Father James what he was. Thea and I had always liked the same people, and now she reminded me of a Gravitron ride I went on once where the ground drops from under your feet, that bizarre and indescribable feeling of the place you always stand falling out beneath you. Half our town reminded me of that now.

Thea studied me for a moment, like she was just noticing something.

"Are you into Elias?" she asked.

Involuntarily, my eyes went to the place where Elias
had sat at my feet. My sister's BS detector, while often
breathtakingly off, could also be shockingly on target. (I
have never met a person who, in some way or other, isn't
a paradox.) But her question made me uncomfortable for
no reason I could say.

"I don't know him," I said.

"He should be careful, with the prank stuff. Isn't he
moving to the city in the fall? A running scholarship?"

"Why?" I asked.

Thea finished chewing a mouthful of tortilla chips.
"Scholarships can be revoked."

Thea and Gabe drove home, but I decided to walk. I
helped get Gabe settled in the car and then nodded to
them and turned back to the park, looking out at the
trees, at the now empty and inviting bowl of grass. I had
it all to myself.

On impulse, I walked to the water's edge and lowered
my towel. My bathing suit was an old one, but it suited

me, navy blue and simple. I felt kind of beautiful as I slid into the water, gripping my way along the side of the falls.

I wasn't trying to swim; I just wanted to feel what it was like to go under the waterfall. I pulled myself along the rocks and behind the churning cascade of cold misty spray. The hollow behind was ever so slightly scary—sort of ancient feeling in the way giant rocky crevices can be.

Standing there, I could picture how easy it might have been for Saint Eia's tribe to see sacredness in streams. It made more sense to me than many things I'd heard at Mary Immaculate. I ran my hands along my goose-bumped arms, touched my fingers to my shivering waist. And then for some goofy reason, I started to sing into the empty cave behind me, listening to my voice echo. It was an old song I remembered my mom singing to me on her rare good days, about pyramids along the Nile and marketplaces in old Algiers. I'd always liked my singing voice, even though I kept it to myself.

And then I looked out through the curtain of water to see a figure at the edge of the bank. I fell silent, mortified, and pulled myself out into the open air.

It was Elias. He was looking at me strangely, with that expression he had when he was thinking of something distracting he wasn't going to tell me. I couldn't tell whether he was embarrassed for me or just generally uncomfortable.

"I came back for my shirt," he said, holding it balled up in his arms.

"You know, you could swim," he added. "You just create momentum with your limbs."

"Wow, with advice like that I wonder why people need swimming lessons."

"I'm glad I found you." He swallowed. "I wanted to tell you something earlier, but not with everyone around."

He looked out toward the street, squinting somewhere. And then his mouth parted in a sly grin.

"I figured out a way to get into the hotel."

If I hadn't been completely engulfed with the awkwardness of the moment, I would have said no. But as it was, I didn't have the space to think.

Elias handed me his shirt, still balled up in his arms, so I could dry myself with it.

"When do we go?" he said. When, not *if.*

Chapter 9

THAT NIGHT WE CROSSED THE NARROW, carved stone bridge that led across the Green Valley River to the Rose grounds, shimmying under its gate on our elbows like Navy SEALs. Elias had found a weakness in the electric fence where it had gotten tangled and lifted in some tree branches on the northeast edge of the property, and that's where we shimmied next. The gap was big and easy to get through, but my heart pounded nearly out of my chest anyway.

"I'm gonna get Lyme disease," I whispered, dragging our ghost-hunting equipment behind me. Elias laughed, too loud.

The skies were still clear enough from the day's weather that we could see the moon three-quarters full above us, its light revealing the wide, expansive, and overgrown property I'd only ever glimpsed from far away. The barbed wire was easy to navigate, having sagged here and there, and soon we were standing on the main part of the grounds: near a gazebo and a gathering of decayed wicker lawn chairs.

The hotel loomed above us beyond the tall grass. Its corners and facade were cast in its own shadow, but I could make out the three main wings, a pointed turret on top of each one, and the shapes of the angels and gargoyles perched on its cornices. A round, empty fountain stood in the courtyard out front, carved with lunging angels. Verandahs, punctuated by stone pillars, swept the front of each floor. The whole place was majestic and impressive but also *off*, with a slightly crooked tilt from being a bit sunken on one side. Perched right on the edge of the rocky gorge of the river, it did give you the feeling it could one day topple in.

We walked closer, Elias getting his equipment ready while I scanned the area for night guards, police lights, security cameras. Elias already knew there were none; he already knew where he was going.

Brazen and relaxed, as if we were on Main Street in the middle of a Saturday, he led me to a corner of the building. Near the dark shadow of an evergreen whose branches were practically stabbing the wall, he pointed to a window— about four feet off the ground—that he'd already found to be unlocked. He hoisted himself up on one of the branches, pulled it open about two feet, and propped it with a stick he already had waiting there. Close up, the building smelled like moldy wet stone, like the old days.

"Everything else I tried was locked," he said. "I haven't been in yet. I wanted to wait for you."

I hesitated.

"I'm good. I'll wait outside," I said, knowing my hesitation would mean nothing to Elias.

He shimmied up and through the window, using the tree as leverage, and disappeared into the dark, his hand emerging a second later to pull me up. I sighed, ignored it and climbed, gripping the branch with one hand and the ledge with the other, my body scraping along the windowsill as I slid in and slipped softly onto the floor beside him. I was scared of everything but that didn't mean I couldn't climb. The sounds of the crickety wet night were swallowed immediately in the stillness of the space. Elias pulled out two flashlights and handed me one. I looked around to see where I'd landed.

Shafts of moonlight fell through the windows, revealing an enormous marble lobby surrounding us under a coffered gold ceiling. At one end of the room was a grand sweeping staircase; and at the other, two smaller stairways led up to the second-level mezzanine that peered down into the open space from behind carved wooden railings. Tables and chairs painted in gold trim were placed neatly around the room and positioned on lush, soft rugs that glittered gold and black in the dark. A dusty grand piano stood in a corner, and three chandeliers dangled above the room. A statue, human-shaped but barely discernible from below, gazed down at us from above the portico of the main double doors. The whole place was treasure-like, kept nostalgic for the bygone era when it was built and now double nostalgic because even the time of its revival was gone.

"I can't believe it's all just . . . sitting here," Elias said.

An enormous gleaming wood bar lined the entire back of the room, with an etched-glass mirror stretching ceilingward behind it. Elias walked behind the bar and tried to flick the lights along the mirror, but of course there was no power.

He leaned his elbows on the bar's dusty surface. I sidled up on a stool.

"The usual?" he asked.

"Make it a double," I said. "I have to spend the night with a paranormal investigator." He shook his head and ducked behind the bar. Then he stood up, looking apologetic.

"What a shame for your friend," he said. "It seems we are out of spirits." Elias raised an eyebrow, pleased with himself.

I shrugged, having found it was better not to encourage him when he was punning. I slid off the barstool and wandered across the foyer. We walked to the towering windows that looked out over the river. We pressed our faces to the glass. You could barely hear the rapids below, the glass was so thick, but we could still see the glistening water deep down in the gorge, which made me a bit dizzy. The turn-of-the-century houses built along the river stood out in the dark, winding their way up the sides of the cliffs. One floor below, there was a wide courtyard with a glass pyramid poking up through the middle, as if to indicate an underground room.

"Let's just prowl around before we start with the

equipment." Elias looked so serious I wanted to laugh, despite my nerves jangling at the whole situation.

The place was enormous, even bigger than it seemed from outside. Down one carpeted hallway we found an empty boutique, a hair salon with sinks and cushioned vinyl chairs, and the entrance to a vast dining room belonging to a restaurant called Tipper's. The tables still had tablecloths, lying under layers of dust. "Not the quality I'm used to at Tipper's," Elias said. I tried to look it up on my phone, to see if Tipper had been a real person, but the whole place seemed to be a cellular dead zone.

A deep alcove off the lobby led down a set of stairs to a huge tiled room holding an underground swimming pool, with a clouded glass pyramid of a sunroof that was the flipside of what we'd seen poking up into the courtyard. From here, a set of stairs led to unlocked doors and the stairway that curled up to Chimney Rise, which was the highest point of the cliffs and had an overlook where people liked to go to make out. Chimney Rise was the kind of ancient geological feature the aliens would find still standing one day when humans had gone extinct.

In other nooks and crannies we found a bank of updated ornate elevators (with bronze-plated doors to keep with the era), a shoeshine stand, a corner fountain of stone cherubs stained by old pennies. There were velvety curtains, enormous vases, paintings of landscapes, an old hand-crank radio with a masking tape label indicating it had belonged to a guy named Stan, who may or may not have been the last concierge. There was no way people outside could have guessed what hidden beauty lay inside the Rose. It felt a million miles away from the rain, the weather, the world. That was the one thing I liked from the start.

Up the grand stairs, my hand traced a path in the dust of the banister that, when I looked back, Elias's hand was following. In the second-floor hall was a row of locked guest rooms with brass number plates, punctuated by black-and-white photos of people who'd stayed here when it was open: George Bush, Michael Jackson, Maya Angelou, Oprah.

The next floor was the same, with lines of guest room doors and photos. But on the top floor there was a difference, something intriguing. A door at the end of the hall was marked Owners' Residence. Elias tried the knob, then stood staring at it.

"That's where the Van Dorens lived," he said. "That's

the place they'd be most likely to haunt." He said this matter-of-factly, as if he were saying, "This is how you change your oil." Frankly, I'd forgotten we were here looking for ghosts at all. He tried the door again, then frowned.

"Well." I looked at him. "Let's start small. Let's search where we can."

We retrieved our equipment from the lobby and began methodically, in the rooms that we did have access to. I mostly just made a show of waving my meter around so that Elias would think I was trying. We did this for two hours all around the lobby, the underground pool, the hallways of the upper floors.

"It's too much to think we'd see them on our first try," Elias finally said, as our night waned. Dawn would be coming in about an hour. We were on the top floor, in a particularly claustrophobic and narrow corner of the hall. I could hear his disappointment more than see it, as my flashlight was trained on the floor.

And then . . . my flashlight went out. I tapped it to try to jog the battery, but nothing. Elias shifted and lifted his, but it flared up for a moment and then also died.

We stood there for a moment in silence. Of course, I knew what was coming.

"They're here," he said.

"Battery fatigue is here," I replied. "You probably put the batteries in at the same time."

"It's a sign."

"There's no such thing as signs."

"We'll have all summer to come back."

That was the thing he said that was most wrong of all. We wouldn't have the summer, in the end.

In truth, we'd only come back for three more visits. After that, for the last time, I'd be alone.

You have to try to picture how a storm grows. It starts as wet warmth floating upward, releasing air as it goes. The air knots around itself, in a twirl, and the more warm water, the more warm air, the bigger the storm. The bigger the storm, the more ocean water it lifts and dumps inland, flooding the waterways in its path. I know this now, though I didn't before. This is how hurricanes are made.

You have to picture how a city of eight million people floods. It starts at the edges.

Sister Suzanne once said she thinks we all add up at the end of a very long, perfect equation that God wrote. She said to find how you got where you are, you have to go backward along it: unraveling where you started, finding what was dropped and added.

And so it's this equation I most need to follow:

The train in the lake.

The smallness of a pinkie touch.

Plus wet air floating to the sky.

Chapter 10

BY MID-JULY THE INSIDES OF GREEN VALLEY'S houses smelled mildewed, and all our clothes felt permanently damp. The grass and bushes and trees grew so green and thick I started to understand how if you lived in the rain forest you couldn't beat nature back unless you made it your full-time job.

There were roadblocks to our return to the Rose: a visit to family friends for Elias and the Khans, a sodden camping trip Gabe insisted we take. Many nights, Elias and I didn't connect.

On the nights we did, the Rose smelled mildewed, too, and its thick rugs felt moist under our feet. Sometimes I could forget that Green Valley had ever had less rain than it did now. Other times the unrelenting gray sky would drive me nuts. Still, for the purposes of Elias and me, it worked: no one was coming out to the Rose in the pouring rain to check for vandals and lurkers. The weather was a veil hiding our nighttime searches like the wall of thorns in "Sleeping Beauty."

The second time we got in, rain pelting the roof, we searched apart but found nothing—though I did sometimes still feel like we were being watched. It was Elias infecting me, I knew.

On our third visit we found the lockbox full of room keys hidden in an alcove in the bar, and it felt like discovering treasure. To Elias, the rooms seemed as good a place as any for the dead to be hiding, though he was crestfallen when it turned out none of the keys fit the door of the owners' residence.

As for the guest rooms, they each looked mostly the same: faded rose-colored carpet, dark glossy wood desks, identical embroidered reading chairs by the windows. My favorite was room 203, a corner room that faced not the river but the fields behind the hotel and the comfort of dry land.

We searched every guest room that third night, like a well-oiled paranormal-seeking machine. Eventually we made our way down to the pool room again, defeated. Elias lifted a pool lounger—a curled *S* made of foam that appeared to be disintegrating—from a bin in the corner and walked into the empty depression of the pool. He lay down on it to pose as if he had a cocktail in his hand; and I joined him, and we pretended to sunbathe for a while.

"I simply can't abide the summer crowds in the north," he said, with an Australian accent layered into a British one.

"We'll go to the Continent in the fall," I replied, lolling my head and blocking the imaginary sun with one hand.

I stole a look at him. There was a sadness on his face. He stood and brushed himself off.

By the time we made it up to the lobby, the heaviness was palpable. I could guess what he was thinking: we hadn't found ghosts . . . and not even a hint of the Van Dorens, in the one place they would be if they were anywhere. As much as I'd always known this was inevitable, I wished it weren't.

We wove our way home in the dark, past Mary Immaculate and the parking lot where we'd first met by the old KISS tree.

We lingered there, looking at the scarred trunk. Years of damage from jaggedly carved names made it look as if the tree was ready to just give up and fall into the water. The land around it and along the edge of the parking lot was eroded by the swollen river, exposing some of its roots.

"I was going to carve Peter Murphy's name that day," I blurted out.

He blinked, remembering. "That kid was an asshole."

"I know."

Elias stared at the tree, his eyes glazed over, maybe from lack of sleep.

"You asked me why I wrote you all those years," he said suddenly. "You know, I'd seen you around that summer, always hanging back but with this intent look on your face—always quiet but pissed off. And then that day, I saw you wait till everyone had left before you climbed. And turned out you could climb higher than any of them." He smiled. "You know what I was thinking?"

I shook my head.

"I was thinking, this world is full of people making a big deal out of any little thing they do: *look at me, look at this cappuccino I'm about to drink, look at me looking good in this hotel lobby.* And here was someone who only did her most beautiful things when no one was watching." He paused. "And you're still like that."

I didn't answer. I felt uncomfortable and flattered at once. He nudged me with his elbow, still looking at the tree. "You're all substance and no style, Cassie Blake. That's why I kept writing to you."

I couldn't think what to say.

"You'd be good at being angry," he said. "You'd get it right."

We were quiet for a long time. I'd read this thing once about fish: in every school of fish there are cautious fish and brave fish, and the school needs them both to survive because the brave fish find food and new places to live but they also get eaten first, and the cautious fish hang back and scope things out and live on to swim another day. It seemed like a bad trade.

I changed the subject. "Peter carved Thea's name up there once, years later. I was so jealous he never carved mine."

"I got you," Elias said simply, abruptly. He turned toward the tree and began to climb.

He was not, as it turned out, a good climber. He was too tall, like the Jolly Green Giant trying to get up a flagpole. Nevertheless, he managed to shoot past all the names. Freeing one hand, he pulled his keys out of his pocket to access a Swiss Army knife he had attached to his key chain. He carved *Cassie* at least two full feet above *Wendy McGowan*. And then he slid back down, getting scraped the whole way. He landed ungracefully and somewhat in pain.

"That's me giving you love," he said. "Purely platonic love right there."

I didn't know why he said it. It was like drawing a line.

This was what I was not guarded against: that there were notes of me only Elias could hear.

One minute you are indifferent to someone else's existence, and the next your entire world is entwined with where they go and what they choose and what could happen to them. And wherever they go, it exposes you, because part of you goes, too, even though it isn't your choice. And sometimes later you wish you could take that connection back, but you can't.

—✳—

"Better luck tomorrow," I said, to be encouraging. "With the ghosts."

Elias looked at me, brightening.

"Tomorrow we have the night off," he said. "Try to sleep. The next day we're doing a *day* thing."

I stared at him and waited.

"What are we doing?"

Elias only shouldered his equipment and beelined for the window. "We'll meet at the KISS tree at nine a.m.," he said. "Think of an excuse."

Gabe was awake when I got home, lying in my bed waiting for me as dawn was creeping in beyond the windows.

"What did you do?" he whispered to me.

"I snuck out," I said, because I was bad at lying, especially to Gabe.

"I want to come with you next time," he said.

"It's not for kids, Gabey."

"Elias likes me better than you," he said.

"Who wouldn't like you better than me? You're awesome."

He nodded, staring at me.

"I promise, sometime we'll take you with us," I said,

119

half lying. *Maybe* we could.

And then he promptly fell back to sleep, seeming to leave it at that. Then again, Gabe contained multitudes.

I crawled in beside him and listened to the birds chirp the world awake. And for a while, I slept.

Chapter 11

TWO DAYS LATER, ELIAS COAXED ME ONTO A
bus and then onto a train to New York City, to see Saint
Eia's golden stone.

On the train, I watched glimpses of the skyline rising up out of the flat vista of the Meadowlands. New
York looked like a sparkling beast slumped in the Hudson
River. It was like you took the train in and it swallowed
you whole . . . no matter that it swallowed you in glitter and Broadway shows and Italian food, you got eaten
nonetheless. I felt a thrill, watching out the windows as
the city rose up closer and closer, and then we disappeared

down into the tunnels that branched under the river and into Manhattan. I'd told my family I'd be at the convent all day; around five, they'd expect me home. I didn't realize I was holding my breath until Elias poked my side and deflated me.

At Penn Station, everything and everyone was impossibly fast. I got knocked around until Elias tugged at my sleeve. "You look like roadkill, mate. Honestly." He gently took my wrist and we moved through the terminal, up a stairway, and out into the city above. We emerged into the wet air and walloping noise of Seventh Avenue and made our way east and then north, past Macy's, banks, souvenir shops, and three Starbucks.

Everything was motion. And then we reached Bryant Park, and to our right the crowds gave way to space and a wide expanse of grass and the imposing sight of the library: infinite-looking stone, sweeping arches. We walked alongside the park, hooking our way around to reach the front entrance. SAINTS IN THE DARK read a banner above the doorway, heralded on either side by medieval-looking angels blowing trumpets.

"Patience and Fortitude," Elias said, pointing to the statues of lions at either side of the doors.

"How do you know?" I asked.

"Well, I'm not ignorant." Which made me realize he'd looked it up on his phone.

Inside, a mix of tourists and locals milled around the enormous foyer, chatting under the arched pillars and domed ceiling.

"You can find anything here," he said, winding us toward the stairs while I dragged my feet. "Old westerns, history, how to make chicken piccata, books of paintings, vintage postcards, stuff about Santa Claus. My uncle brought me here, that summer I visited."

The exhibit was on the second floor, beyond a doorway with banners on either side of it, adorned with paintings of a man and a woman with golden halos looking toward the stars. Beyond the doorway they'd done something cool with the lighting so that the room was dim, illuminated only with tiny lights from above.

I didn't get how an enormous city could have such quiet corners. Specially lit shelves ran the length of the room. I ran my gaze along the spines of the books, which were like the ones we'd inherited for the convent library: mostly printed a long time ago, a lot of plain covers embossed with gold. There were also sacred objects tucked safely inside ornate gold reliquaries, which were themselves housed in protective glass cases.

A placard explained how the relics were classified:

Third-class relics had touched a saint, or had touched something belonging to a saint.

Second-class relics had actually *belonged* to a saint.

First-class relics were actually a *piece* of the saint, like a bone or a lock of hair.

"You cannot make this shit up," Elias said.

We stared at the enclosed scraps of cloth, a vial of dried blood, a couple of mummified fingers, a silver necklace. Catholics were weird, like Elias said—much as I'd always taken it all for granted. But I'd be lying if I said it didn't feel like some kind of magician's closet.

Each glass case had an alarm and a single bright white light trained on it from above. And there, under one of the lights, inside an open gold box on top of a small velvet pillow, was a glittery lump of rock. My pulse quickened. I walked up to it and read the small plaque on the side of the glass. *The Sacred Stone of Saint Eia, Second-Class Relic.* I stared at it.

Elias stood beside me, giving off an air of dutiful seriousness. After we stared at it for a suitable amount of time, he impatiently nudged me.

"What do you think?"

"I don't know," I said. It looked vaguely like a chicken nugget.

Had it really been hers? Had *she* even been a living, breathing person? I couldn't imagine it. I tried to envision her actual hands holding it, that her real fingers had touched it. I tried to imagine seeing the world and the rock the way she had, full of powers we can't see. I couldn't quite fathom it. It wasn't like I'd expected it to levitate or anything. I just couldn't quite make the leap to Saint Eia ever being alive and in the flesh.

Elias nudged me again. "C'mon. I wanna show you something else."

He took me up the stairs into a beautiful painted foyer and led me into the room beyond. *This* room was almost as big as a football field, with enormous windows stretching top to bottom and a ceiling painted with clouds full of pinks and yellows and blues. There were ladders everywhere for reaching the highest bookshelves. People sat at desks, studying and reading and tapping on laptops.

I smelled the book air. I listened to the book sounds that went deeper than silence. It felt like the books swallowed the quiet and turned something back on you that wasn't quite quiet at all.

Elias watched my face. "It's great, right?" He bounced

on the balls of his feet, restless. "Oh, and this is cool. The *Oxford English Dictionary.*" He leaned over a lectern holding the biggest book I'd ever seen. I walked up beside him and gazed down at the open page, squinting at the crowded type. "It's nuts. I watched this boring movie about it once and then shut the movie off halfway and looked it up online instead. All these random people would mail in little slips of paper with examples of the ways words could be meant. The word *set* has like four hundred meanings."

He paged forward, and then pointed to one of the many definitions under *tarantula.* "'Tarantula. An insect whose bite is only cured by musick.'"

I turned to the *A*s and scanned a random page. "'Anatiferous. Producing ducks.'"

Elias paused like he was considering. "Makes sense."

The whole book was sweet, and gigantic, and weird.

"There's no need for any other book but this one," Father James used to say to us in eighth-grade confirmation class, holding up a Bible. I thought about how there were the people in the world who felt so certain about things, and then there were others sending in four hundred definitions of the word *set* just so you could see it in a million tiny shades of gray. And I couldn't help thinking that it was the shades-of-gray people who felt, to me, like home.

It was exquisite. Or maybe that was just the feeling Elias left behind him. Maybe he made everything feel exquisite, including me. I once thought it was exquisite that he added avocados to a salad.

When I dream about Elias, I dream we are in this room.

On the train home, I laid my head on his shoulder. It was the first time we'd touched that closely. I realized that, much against my own better judgment, I was in love with him. It was something that I couldn't help. I tried to keep my breathing slow and easy so that he'd believe I was asleep.

He laid his head against mine, and I wondered if he was pretending too.

Chapter 12

IT WAS OUR LAST NIGHT IN THE ROSE HOTEL, though we didn't know it.

Elias had brought a crowbar to pry open the door to the owners' residence, but he was better at dressing like a cat burglar than actually having burglar skills. And so we were finally out of places to look for ghosts.

Elias looked glum, like his restlessness had drained out of him. I made a show for a while of setting up our recording devices, but my heart wasn't in it. Finally I laid my equipment down and padded up the stairs. I walked into room 203, still my favorite, gazing at the view of the field and the rain. Elias walked in behind me and threw himself on the bed. I glanced back at him, and he patted the space beside him.

I went and sat down on the mattress and then eased myself onto my back by his side, keeping my eyes on the window. I turned my back to him, and in another moment, he rolled to drape his arm across me and nestle behind me.

I lay still as I could, like a rabbit when it senses a change in the air. But if Elias was thinking of anything but hugging a friend, he didn't show it. He seemed ready to doze off.

"You're warmer than me," I said.

"You've got the circulation of a vampire," he answered. "This is well documented."

Meanwhile, I hoped he couldn't hear the pounding of my heart. He still smelled like the woods.

"My parents called," he said. "We're losing our apartment. Three months behind on rent."

I rolled onto my back again and turned my head to look at him.

"I'm so sorry," I said. "Where will they go?"

"I don't think they know," he said. "They might go back to Western Australia. They might go stay with my aunty in Melbourne. Sometimes they talk about starting over and trying to make a go of it in Bangladesh near my grandmother's family, I think that's always been a pull. But if you think *Australia*'s experiencing a cornucopia of delights thanks to the weather changing . . ." He trailed off. "It breaks your heart." He scratched at his hair again, like he was itching to get out of his skin. "My parents count on me making my future in school here. And all I want to do is spend my time on ghosts."

He closed his eyes and got quiet. His breathing became steady. This lasted for several minutes. I thought he'd fallen asleep, but when I glanced over at him again, he was looking at me.

"Why can't you sleep, Cassie?"

I blinked at him. And then I almost laughed. He'd been sneaking it up on me all this time. *Whatever I'm doing, I've already started doing it.* He was trying to therapize me out of my insomnia.

"I don't know." I looked up at the ceiling. "When we were kids, before my mom left, it was like, I thought someone was taking care of things, you know? But now I feel like if I fall asleep, nobody's flying the plane. It's like I've got to stay awake to keep the plane up in the air."

Elias listened but didn't say anything. I didn't know if I

was making sense. He cleared his throat.

"Remember those boys who got stuck in that cave in Thailand? There was . . . like . . . a two percent chance of getting them out, but people just went for it anyway. And they got them. I mean, they swam through all these gnarly caves in the dark and got them. I think that's the way to believe in something." He shifted on his pillow, resting a hand under his cheek as he looked at me. "Like, you do all this work toward something that may turn to shit, and you try to fix something it may not be possible to fix. You just take off and hope."

For some reason, this made me want to cry. Because I wanted to do what he was saying. And I also couldn't imagine it. I was a damn cautious fish.

Then, with a sigh, he slid his arm away from me. I felt his warmth slip from mine. He stood and went to the desk. He slid out a piece of hotel stationery and a pen from one of the drawers. He leaned over the desk and wrote.

"I'm writing a secret," he said. "Something big, something you'd really want to know. Something that could change your life." He straightened up and looked back at me.

"Close your eyes," he said, doing that up-and-down

thing he did, that restless slight bouncing on the balls of his feet that made him look eight and not eighteen.

He pointed with two fingers at his eyes, then mine. I let my lids drop shut.

I heard his footsteps leaving the room. I supposed he thought maybe I could see through walls, so I kept my eyes closed. He was gone for several minutes, and either he was quiet as a jewel thief or he'd gone somewhere far.

And then I heard him slide against the door and reappear. I looked up at him.

"There," he said. "Now you just have to look for it."

"What's the point of hiding something for me that I'll never find?" I asked flatly.

"Faith," he said.

"That's so dumb," I replied.

Elias was undeterred.

"Think about our secrets. The things only you and me were there for. That's your free clue."

He climbed back onto the bed with me and wrapped his arm over me. And then, while I listened to his breathing and felt every place his body touched mine with a kind of ache like he was already gone, he fell asleep for real.

—✳—

There was no way I'd ever find it, for so many reasons. But I promised myself I'd come back and look for Elias's paper. I didn't care what he was trying to prove to me. I just wanted to know what it said.

I lay awake, listening to the sounds of the hotel. I found myself waiting, listening now, for anything that sounded like movement, feeling for chills in the air, for almost imperceptible moans in the dark.

I realized why I'd been nervous at the trestle bridge, and was nervous now. There was the smallest part of me, maybe a 2 percent part, that had changed because of him, that was afraid there were ghosts around the room, haunting us after all. Which was actually no small amount when you compared it to zero.

A few days later, Elias was caught in the act. The irony was, it was probably the funniest prank.

He had found an unlocked bathroom window at the priests' residence and dressed a mannequin as Saint Patrick: with a felt beard, a tan sheet as a robe, and a felt shamrock taped to his hand. Elias had loaded it through the window and onto the floor facedown. The idea was that it would look like a Saint Patrick crime scene. In any case, Father Bob walked into the bathroom just as Elias was crawling out the window, and thought they were being robbed, and had a "minor cardiac event."

Elias had always been meticulous in his timing. I guessed he was sleep-deprived and because of that, sloppy. Or maybe he was tired of hiding his tracks.

That was how the summer of Father James pranks came to an end. It was like Le Tits Now times ten . . . and in normal times, it would have been punished accordingly, and no more than that. But these were not normal times.

Chapter 13

CHURCH WAS SO HUMID THAT GABE HAD laid himself down along the cool wooden pew for relief. The adults were fanning themselves with their pamphlets. The boring bits had been gotten through and everyone was rustling with anticipation for Father James's sermon like we were waiting to watch gladiators at the Colosseum. You could tell it was gonna be one for the ages.

The priest stood at the lectern, his hands gripping the sides.

He warmed up with some denouncements of the latest restrictions being placed on the Skyline View, which was almost finished. He graciously thanked the parents and families who had made the toy drive such a success. He mentioned that only people who ignored Scripture would vote for Jasmine Lovell for mayor. And finally, he got to Elias.

"Now, some of you in the community know that our church has been the target of a series of malicious pranks," he said. A few parishioners nodded. "There are people in our midst who hate what we stand for. And there are shepherds of this flock who would tell you to ignore this ugliness among us. Well, I'm not one of them."

Looking around nervously at some of those who were nodding, I was awed by how he'd managed to wrap enough of the congregation around him so tightly that his hurts were their hurts, that attacks on *him* were attacks on them.

"I'm just the messenger on this, my friends. I don't know how people do it in other parts of the world. But those who can't respect our values have *no* place here. And I'd be happy to personally escort them to the nearest airport."

There was a rustle as several people nodded emphatically. I felt sick to my stomach. Thea gave me a side-eye, but I couldn't read what it meant. I couldn't tell if she, too, thought Elias hated God and churches and priests instead of just one priest who was an asshole.

Then Father James smiled, the kind of smile that lets you know you are on the same *good* team. "By the way, I don't know if you all have tried Cookie Caverns in East Township. I've heard it's dirty." His smile crooked up on one side but didn't reach his eyes. "Perhaps the next prank is bugs in your birthday cake."

A year before, people would have seen this for the soft-footed hatred it was. But now, Father James simply moved on to other things, and after church, people just milled around in the parish hall over the cake and coffee and chatted as usual like frogs on a hot pan. Meanwhile, my feet felt numb, and I kept my mouth shut.

The fallout was subtle, but swift.

People who used to trek over to the Khans' bakery for their bagels and black-and-white cookies stopped going. When it came time for the mid-August Mary Immaculate picnic, which the Khans usually catered, they weren't asked. Most people our age didn't change much, though for the real Father James loyalists like Thea, Elias was less golden than he had been. She and her friends stopped talking about him so much and kept a distance from him at the park.

All it was, Thea said, was words; an opinion about a bakery was meaningless. "It has nothing to do with Father James," she said, when I pressed her on it. "People just want to blame him for stuff." We left it at that, staying away from the land mines. You couldn't say it had anything to do with them being Khans instead of O'Connells, or that they were part Bangladeshi or part Australian or that Mrs. Khan was into new age goddesses, or anything specific. But you couldn't say it didn't, either. People use poison because it's invisible.

And I saw, with a nauseating, weightless feeling, that the surest way you got people to hate people was convincing them they were hated first.

That's how a golden boy who did harmless pranks and believed in ghosts turned from a local darling into an enemy as the summer wound down. By that time, *every-one* who was not us was an enemy, thanks to a year of letting Father James leverage our fear, and the weather woven underneath it.

It moved through me like a fever. My town was my bones, the roots that fused my bones together. My town was me; this was the problem.

Elias, meanwhile, was grounded for life. Or at least until he left for school.

But later that week, I got a letter from him, mailed from down the street.

> *Thursday night. Meet me at the KISS tree. We*
> *need to do one last thing.*

I stared at the letter and the million possibilities of the last thing we might do fluttered through my mind, soft and ticklish as the wing of a bee.

Chapter 14

THURSDAY NIGHT, I READ *GOODNIGHT MOON* to Gabe and Barney, who was sleeping over, and I watched the clock. Dad was away for a couple of nights to help my aunt move, and Thea was in her room watching TV.

Gabe and I both agreed that *Goodnight Moon* was the best book ever written. It was about a rabbit going to sleep and wishing good night to everything from his mush to the air to nobody to some mittens. Reading *Goodnight Moon* was the most sleeplike experience you could get without sleeping, which was appealing to someone like me. On the other hand, Barney said it was for babies.

Tonight, the boys could not sit still for it. They

burrowed into my closet and pulled out Gabe's backpack to go through his latest drawings. (Gabe's people were always armless and perfectly happy; it was like he just hadn't noticed arms yet.) They kept stealing my phone and telling Siri to play a terrible album called *Essential Kidz Toonz*, snorting at my annoyance.

I thought they might never fall asleep, but finally, close to 10:00, they did, curled like two little larvae under my blankets.

I switched over to Saint Eia, which I'd set aside for a long while, just then deep in her journey toward the sea in search of the Vandals. Around this part, she lost hope she'd ever reach her golden stone at all and got a bit psychotic about it. She painted her face in the blood of her enemies.

Thea turned out her light at about 11:00.

Around 1:30 I checked in on everyone to make sure they were still asleep and that Thea's door was open in case the boys woke and needed help. And then I pulled on my sneakers and walked outside. If there was a rustle behind me of two small heads rousing to see me go, I didn't hear it.

It was one of those late-August nights with a hint of fall in the air, a touch of coolness floating on the breeze.

Elias was standing under the tree, looking at the river, which was particularly wild and wavy tonight, churning up everything in its path. The parking lot was inundated with standing water along its edge. The sky was cloudy but miraculously dry.

He had all his equipment beside him: every infrared sensor, ghost box, and laser grid I had ever seen him lug somewhere. He turned to look at me.

And from his look I knew, knew in my bones, it would be our last night together.

"Elias," I said.

"It was totally funny until it wasn't," he said. "And then the cops arrived."

I walked up beside him and stood shoulder to shoulder with him, and we both looked out at the water. I could picture him laughing to himself in his overconfident way as he climbed through the window of the priests' residence, dragging the mannequin in behind him.

"It's weird," he said, not meeting my eyes. "I can't read people. I can't tell who still likes me and who doesn't. It's like with each person I know, I have to read some invisible bubble above their heads." He let out a long breath. "My aunty and uncle say people are batshit everywhere but there's a special brand of American crazy."

"He'll go away eventually," I said. I didn't have to say who.

"Fuck me. My country is on fire, and my aunt's farm in Bangladesh is getting eaten by the sea, and people like him are just pointing anywhere but at the ground under our feet. And for some reason people think that makes sense. There's a million guys where he came from, and people *love* these guys. What do you do with that?" he said.

I took this in and felt foolish. I had no idea what to do with it. Anyway, I'd always thought Elias was just a brave guy gunning for an asshole. I realized now it had always been personal.

"My aunty's supervigilant now, and even *the coin collecting show* isn't enough. I can't risk it anymore, sneaking out. If I get sent home, my future is fucked. Not to mention I'd probably never see you again. Not till we're like, thirty, which is how long it'd take me to save up for a flight, and by then we'll be driving SUVs and I'll have a dad bod."

"Not unlikely," I said. Trying not to sound devastated.

We might see each other during the day before he left for school, but we'd never have a night again.

"I think this is it for us, our last chance."

He looked up at me, and I felt a prickling along my neck. And then he smiled. "Or we could run away," he said, his mouth tilting at one corner. "We could go do something forever."

I felt my breath leave me. "Where would we go?"

He searched his mind. "The moon."

I smiled. I pictured us on the moon. It felt on the edge of things that neither of us wanted to say.

"The moon sounds like a safe bet," I said.

"Yeah. But you've already got so much safety you're choking on it." He bit his lip at the last words, like they had just slipped out. And again, my breath whooshed out of me.

"Anyway, it's our last chance to do this." He lifted the laser grids and tossed them and the EMF meters into the water below. I let out an involuntary yelp.

Before I could say anything, he threw in the sensor, too, then tilted his head and looked at me, surprised by my reaction. "I'm done with ghosts," he said, as if I should already know that, holding his wrist recorder out over the water. "I'm never going to find them. This is absurd; why didn't you ever tell me this was absurd?" He dropped the recorder. It went plummeting into the river and bobbed a moment before disappearing into the wild foam. And there it was: the heavy thing and the light all over his face.

"You don't have to pollute the river," I said, trying to stop his hand.

"I don't care."

"You could sell that stuff for money," I pressed.

Suddenly, Elias paused. He looked down into the water, too late. "I didn't think of that."

We were quiet for a long time. My heart thumped in a slight panic. If Elias stopped believing in magical things, someone like me would have no hope. But I didn't say it. That was a lot of pressure to put on a person.

The woods were loud around us, nature talking about itself like all the summer's rain had multiplied the crickets and tree frogs to millions. We watched the river for any sign of what Elias had thrown in, but it was all long gone now.

"Do you think I just imagined it, that day?"

He was shivering and staring at me, as if my opinion meant more to him than anything. I held out my arms, then dropped them at my sides.

We looked at each other, empty-handed.

"I should get back," he said, looking around nervously.

I nodded, trying to quell the rising loss, the looming goodbye that felt like panic. My lungs felt suddenly small and all I needed was air I couldn't get.

We walked through the scrubby woods alongside the river, away from the lights of the parking lot and into the glade. Here the sounds of the night creatures were deafening.

We were in the clearing of the meadow when it happened.

I understood the science of it later, when I heard about it on the local news.

An intense zone of rising air had thrown water vapor high into the sky, where it condensed, froze, and came down again. Meteorologists called it a splash event. The tiny crystals must have started out enormous to make it down to us through the heat. It was a freak moment of nature, in a year of freak weather.

"Holy shit," Elias said, looking up.

And though it was August, and hot enough to make us sweat, it began to snow.

We both stood in shock for a few moments, not quite

getting what we were seeing. And then Elias held out his hand to catch snowflakes, the tiny white puffs melting even before they touched his hand. We both looked up at the clouds. My mind raced to what might have caused it.

Elias dropped down to do a snow angel even though there wasn't any snow on the ground. I laughed, then dropped beside him to do the same. We waggled our arms and legs wildly for a few minutes, and then, exhausted, lay still. We were lying out flat next to each other, arms outstretched. The trees, the grass, the ground felt alive, and I felt pagan for sure, like just one of the many living things in the woods.

I knew Elias's hand lay just beside mine. This was the moment, the kind of moment that felt like the world created it to give you a push. And tomorrow things would be different.

It was a matter of inches. It was only the slightest and smallest movement in the world, but also irrevocable. I willed myself to do it, but my body stayed frozen. I only let the side of my hand—just the pinkie—brush against his. He didn't even seem to notice.

And then, in another moment, the snow stopped. It just *evaporated* in the air. It had lasted maybe all of two minutes. Elias slid his hand from where it lay, inward against his chest, onto his ribs. I froze, like if I just stayed still enough I could dissolve.

The moment passed me by.

Eventually, he rolled onto his side and looked at me. I stayed where I was, staring at the sky, bereft. And then I stood up to walk. He walked behind me. And then tugged at the back of my shirt to stop me.

I stopped but didn't turn.

"Do you really want to be a nun?" he asked. I looked at him.

And then, for the first and only time, Elias broke a promise to me.

My pulse galloped off like a horse. He appeared to be trembling.

Behind me was a huge knotty tree. Elias slid his hand to my waist, pressing me slowly back against it. He wrapped both hands over the bones at my hips, and lowered his head, leaning his face gently against my collarbone, breathing, before he brought his lips to mine.

He ran nervous hands along my body like he'd been dying to do it all along, and everywhere they touched lit me up. He pulled back to look me in the eyes, the serious and playful thing mixed on his face, and on reflex I pulled off my shirt in a thoughtless swoop, to bring his fingers closer.

We burned so bright I felt like we must glow, a flare of energy in the dark. One brave boy, one cautious fish in the wild, living woods.

And then in another moment I was rolling myself out and away from him, scrambling away from the tree.

My shirt was somewhere on the ground and I crossed my arms over my bra.

"Do you love me?" he whispered. He sounded afraid. He'd been afraid of me all along, I realized.

"I can't," I breathed. Two words to cover everything: how scary it was to know he loved me back; the terror of trading one thing that was perfect for another that was unknown. How do you make yourself braver than you are?

I don't know how much time had slipped past us staring at each other when we heard the sound like a crack of thunder, and a shriek.

Even without seeing, we knew terror when we heard it.

We ran back the way we'd come and came up short on the verge of the parking lot, but couldn't recognize what we saw.

The edge of the lot had unmoored itself from the saturated ground along the roiling river. We watched in shock as small trees were carried into the churning current, roots thrust into the air like fingers clawing for something.

And then again the scream, an animal screech, and near the bobbing trees two shapes in the water. Two small heads and arms flailing before they went under. Two small spies who thought they were ninjas.

Elias was in the water before I could comprehend it. I ran up and down the side like a stupid animal that cannot swim as he paddled toward them frantically.

All along the water, the screams had woken those in nearby houses, sending floodlights pouring onto lawns. The night grew suddenly bright; figures rushed along the edge of the water.

One of the boys washed against the river's edge and scrambled up onto a fallen tree. I could see the dark flash of Barney's hair. The other shape vanished in the rapids, disappearing under a boulder that breached the water, the current foaming over and around it. I moaned, frantic. He'd be lodged beneath it, crushed by the water's force.

Elias went down after him, and everything was silent. They were submerged so long I knew they were gone.

Moments passed, and then more. It was too much time, and too late.

And then Elias exploded up out of the water, gasping for breath.

With one small, limp person in his arms.

Chapter 15

IT WAS A SUMMER IN WHICH WE'D HAD sixty-four inches of rain. The river had risen ten feet and would rise still more before the year was through, though we didn't know that then. The boys were walking on the edge of the asphalt lot, trailing us into the woods, when it dissolved underneath them.

There were proper terms for the disaster. It was a confluence of weather and a weakness in the subgrade that came together to make the land they were standing on crumble. It was, like all true things, complicated.

But it was the hard-to-pin-down things, the in-between things, that were dangerous. No golden hammer . . . just a piling up of small facts. And so Green Valley's anger coalesced most around the simple and half-baked things instead: a girl with no shirt, a boy who pranked priests and roamed the streets in the dark. I was supposed to be watching the boys. Elias was supposed to be home in his bed.

Still. Gabe survived. Gabe survived. *Gabe survived.*

The part of him that got trapped in the rocks, the bones had been not just broken but crushed. His tibia, his ankle, the tiny bones in his left hand. He had four pins put in his wrist. Another five in his leg.

I remember my dad's figure filling up the doorway of the hospital waiting room, his hair framed in the fluorescent light behind him like a halo, wearing a look of such rage I couldn't say I was sorry because I couldn't speak.

In Gabe's hospital bed, on the nights I took my shifts, I'd curl up beside him and soak him in: the smell of him and feel of him, this little person who I couldn't fathom the absence of. I felt an insanely wild hope for him entwined with a beast devouring my chest. I'd used to wish for things like a pet parrot or to live in a tree house. Now I wished I could trade with my brother so I could be the one with broken bones and pins. The relief that he

was still here nearly knocked me over, followed by the
equally earthshaking guilt.

An accumulation of warmer-than-average days carried us
into the end of August and through the four weeks till
Gabe came home.

Barney escaped with a few scratches and nightmares
and the eternal hatred of his parents for me. Around town,
I tried to shrink myself smaller than I ever had, be *even
more* unnoticeable. But invisibility was impossible now;
everyone we knew stared at me like I was a new kind of
human. I hardly left the house, mostly because I wasn't
allowed. I was on house arrest, phone confiscated, forbid-
den from talking to Elias ever again.

My father and Thea sought solace in their faith. They
prayed like their lives depended on it. They prayed to for-
give me, most of all.

With Elias, it was different. A feather could have tipped
our town against him. A half-naked girl and a nearly
drowned child was a battering ram. Father James's words
had seeped into the groundwater. And by the time people
made up their minds about what had really happened by

the river that night, they thought their opinions had just risen up in them like common sense.

Elias's scholarship was a no-brainer. Several people contacted the admissions office to complain. In a matter of a week, the scholarship evaporated.

What was more complicated was that our town was no longer any kind of real place for the Khans. Elias had saved Gabe's life, but people liked to pick their truth instead of the other way around.

And so, while some friends rallied around them, the Khans had had it with the growing atmosphere of our "batshit town." Mr. Khan said Green Valley had turned into that M. Night Shyamalan movie where the people pretend they live in the 1800s and hide from monsters. I heard this from Thea, who heard it from Kelsey, who heard it from God knows where.

Quietly, so quiet that in my fog of days and nights caring for Gabe I didn't see it coming, the Khans drove Elias to Newark Airport and sent him home. He slipped out of my world without me even knowing it until days after he was gone.

The Khans listed their house two weeks later, and the

real estate market being what it was, they apparently got fifty over asking. They moved before I came up for air, to a town upstate where they could still commute to the bakery. When I tried to call them at Cookie Caverns to ask about reaching Elias, they told me it was better if we weren't in touch. And I couldn't blame them: for one thing they didn't know me, had never even met me. And then they stopped answering my calls altogether.

And so, I could only wait for his letters, in the end. And as the weeks passed, the weather still too warm and wet into the early fall, I realized they weren't going to come.

I found out quickly that Elias's online footprint was not just subnuclear but nonexistent.

I went deep: scouring images online, social media pages of random people who shared his name (turns out, the world is full of Elias Joneses), every platform known to God and man, but nothing.

Elias had disappeared into the unknown cartoon world of endless parched landscapes I'd never see. He was drifting around somewhere in Australia without an apartment or a farm to live on, and I was where I was supposed to be: in Green Valley for life. In a big world it was just two people losing track of each other; it happened all the time. But a rage I hadn't felt since childhood came back to me, for Gabe's precious bones and Elias's blank blotch of a future. It swallowed me up. There was no place to get away from it; it was windowless, doorless.

At dinner my dad and Thea circled hands with me to pray, and I stared at the table.

And no one blamed Father James at all.

As if words didn't make the world.

Chapter 16

I BARELY NOTICED FALL AS IT ARRIVED.

I did the easy commute to college, helped Gabe with his therapies in the afternoon (he'd have to *work* to walk, which crushed my heart), and did my homework when everyone slept. I forgot Saint Eia all those weeks, but in early October, when I finally gave up curling up with Gabe in his room every night, I remembered the book and finished it.

The tribe Saint Eia pursued from Rome, the Vandals who'd bought her treasure, evaded her. Ultimately, they crossed the sea, and Saint Eia had no ship.

When she knew that all was lost, she came to the edge of the ocean and—*relicless*—thought about flinging herself in. Her goddesses had abandoned her, if they'd ever been real at all.

This is when God spoke to her, in the form of an angel. He said that if she only followed Him, He'd give her something far greater than what she'd lost.

I don't know why she believed that, or how it all worked out. The story ended with her floating away on the leaf. It didn't say where she ended up, or if she was okay, or if she ever found what she was looking for.

And then, in early November, I heard they'd set a date to demolish the Rose. It was structurally unsound, an eyesore, and a waste of public space. It was also my last chance.

And so, nearly three months after I'd last been there, wanting the last piece of Elias I could have, I went to the hotel to find what he'd left me: the piece of paper he'd said would change my life. By then, the storm was already fanning its edges over the Northeast. In the days ahead of landfall, a storm like that begins to be visible from space.

You have to try to think about it like this: in a time when everything goes haywire, the world can be one thing, and then just a little while later it can be something else. It happens when you blink.

Part
2

Chapter 17

DAWN IS BREAKING WHEN I PULL UP TO THE hotel gate on my bike, the clouds over Cub Mountain golden, with pink at the edges.

According to the news, a storm, Hurricane Kirk, is headed up the Atlantic, far from us. It'll bring rain, which is nothing new. The only thought I give it is that Hurricane Kirk sounds like a very swift, exotic male dancer. There's a breeze, the kind of breeze that comes from some weather drama far away, where the leaves twirl in a way that makes you notice if you're paying attention. Naturally, I haven't slept.

I hide my bike behind a tree. My family will think I'm studying at Nelson Library on campus. At the bridge, I shimmy under the main gate, then navigate the weak spots of the two fences to reach the tall, cool, wet grass of the grounds.

I rise to my feet and, looking around, shiver at the prospect of breaking and entering without Elias. But I am not the me I used to be. I'm *half-missing*, and maybe it's the rule-following half.

I find our window unlocked just as we left it. I brace my foot against the tree branch. I scramble through the gap, and then I'm in.

The lobby feels gloomy now without anyone breathing in it besides me. It also looks transformed in the daylight, the morning revealing the shabbiness of the faded couches, the cracks in the wallpaper. Still, I see things I've never noticed in the dark: gold scrollwork over the entrance, words etched in the top of the glass at the bar (*Good friends, good food, good company*), intricate patterns on the mezzanine railing I never made out in the dark.

"Hello, I'm here," I say, to no one.

I listen to the silence and stare around, and it hits me like a gut punch: Elias has set an impossible task. The lobby alone is three times the size of my house. The odds of my finding a piece of paper folded into the size of a matchbook, when it could be anywhere in this entire hotel, are basically nil. Not to mention that for all I know he could have put it on the roof.

"Think about our secrets. The things only you and me were there for."

I look at my phone to gauge the number of hours I have until dusk. And then I start carefully and methodically.

I search under vases, in the glasses tucked in the bar, beneath couches, under the lid of the piano. I scour the cabinets by the concierge station, pausing when I hear a distant engine roar, certain it's the demolition crew come early. But it's coming from somewhere far away. I peer into the nooks and crannies of statues, in windowsills, in the tucks behind curtains.

I start out planning to tackle the ground level and work upward from there, but by eleven I'm moving back and forth between the floors, realizing it's impossible to cover any space thoroughly. I find curious mementos and left-overs stuffed into drawers and lying under furniture: a black wig, fingernail clippers, an opal ring, a set of XL silk leopard-print pajamas, a hammer . . . but no note.

Lunchtime finds me in the lobby. In silence, I eat a

sandwich I've brought as I sit nestled onto a couch with my knees to my chest, staring out the window toward the river. I watch birds flocking ahead of fluffy white clouds, spilling like ink across the sky. I keep thinking I've seen the last of them, but more keep coming into view, until it seems there might be thousands of them. I watch them go and feel a chill run across me, like when something nags at you that you've forgotten. My mind is somewhere else.

I swallow my last bite and climb back upstairs to keep searching.

I'm coming out of room 405 when I see it.

Two doors down, at the end of the hall, the Van Dorens' door looks as impenetrable as ever, but now I glimpse something in the daylight I never would have noticed in the dark. The moment seems to stand still. I feel chills down my arms.

There—on the top of the doorframe, tilted so that it rests catty-corner and secure—is an edge of something. I leap up and swat the wall above the door so that it comes tumbling down onto the carpet.

I stare at it, dumbfounded. A *key.* I let out something between a cough and a laugh. I pick it up, try it, and find it goes into the lock as easily as butter.

And just like that, I let myself in. For the moment, I forget Elias's note. I forget everything but ghosts.

Inside, it looks like the Van Dorens just left yesterday.

I'm in a kind of apartment. To the left there's a small kitchen with plates and glasses piled up neatly on the counter, a fridge, a stove. There's a vacuum cleaner in one corner, and books perched on a coffee table in front of a couch.

I walk deeper in and find four bedrooms. Thinking back I remember there were three teenagers, two girls and a boy, and it's easy to see whose room is whose, with magazines piled up on the dressers, framed photos, books. It's too eerie, everything frozen in time.

On a table by the window are photos of the family together: a smiling, bearded dad; a mom in a long white dress who looks loving enough never to run off to Ohio; a teenage boy slouching with annoyance; the sisters with their arms linked around each other and sunglasses resting on the tops of their heads. They look like friendly people who didn't want to die.

I follow a set of stairs to a small, sloped-roof room tucked up into what must be the east turret of the building.

There's a little hand-carved wooden sign on the wall that calls it the Crow's Nest. From here there's a postcard view of downtown: Main Street straight ahead, the river to my left and the buildings and houses snaking up along the gorge around it. The prettiest is a brick house with bright blue shutters, and beyond its roof I can just make out the dark glimmer of the reservoir dam. To the right, there's Chimney Rise and the stairs leading to it from the lowest part of the hotel.

I sit on a stool by the window, taking in the view. I'm so tired. I could sleep forever and still never feel up to the task of being awake. In my worst moments, when I'm up wondering if Gabe will ever be the same, if my town will ever be the same, I could sink to the bottom of the sea.

Outside, the first raindrops, very light, begin to fall.

I move down to sit on the carpet and lean back against the wall. I don't mean to close my eyes, but I do. And a year piles up behind my eyelids. And like Rip Van Winkle, I sleep.

Chapter 18

"WAKE UP."

I jerk upright in panic, hearing the voice. Whoever's said it, I can't see them in the dark.

In the dark.

I blink myself awake. My eyes try to focus, but I can only see blackness, no moonlight coming through the window.

A cop, I think, fumbling for my cell phone flashlight. A construction worker.

But as I flick the light, I see no one is there.

Shit.

The dark.

I know what's happened. I've crashed out, several nights of wakefulness catching up with me. And the day has slipped away.

It takes a moment for my astonishment to pass and become concern.

I look at my cell phone again. And a heavy leaden rock thumps in my stomach as I see the time: 1:33 a.m.

I leap to my feet. I snatch my backpack up onto one shoulder and stumble into a corner, still half out of it. And that's when I register the wind, how it's rattling the window.

I grope my way out into the hall, looking down onto the foyer from the balcony, strobing my cell light across the grand piano and the tables. No doubt my dad and Thea are awake back home, the lights of our house blazing as they wait for me to show up. I'm sure they've tried to call, but they wouldn't have gotten through. They must be frantic. Maybe they're letting Gabe sleep so he won't worry; at least I hope they are. No doubt they've called the cops.

My stomach churns hotly. I picture them scared and angry.

I hurry downstairs and across the lobby to the window,

where the tree is swaying back and forth so much, I can't make sense of it. In seconds, I climb and squeeze out through the gap and land on the grass with a thud.

It's raining hard. Wind lifts my hair. I turn and squint into the dark, and realize just how sheltered I've been from the weather; it's louder and windier than I imagined from inside. There's no moon. The air is saturated; it smells like the sea. Something's rattling along the grass but I can't see what. And then I remember the hurricane. It must be passing closer than expected.

I'm just pivoting on my heels to head for the bridge when something streaks along the corner of my vision and whops me. I fall sideways, whacking my head against the wall under the window. A flash of light streaks through my vision and leaves a halo of light buzzing behind my eyes.

I see it's Elias's branch that's the culprit.

"Traitor," I gasp. And then "*Shit.*"

I'm so dizzy from the impact I can barely stand straight.

"*Shit.*" I think how I'm going to end up in one of those newspaper columns about criminals being idiots: how I'll be caught by the demolishers lying here in the grass because I've knocked myself unconscious.

Walking at an angle because the world keeps tilting,

I hurry to the fence and come to a dead stop. A few feet ahead, I see the bridge is submerged, inches of water washing over it.

I stare at it, disbelieving. Has the rain made the river rise so quickly? Is it something with the distant storm, pushing water inland? Is that a thing?

I watch the water rushing past and recount the world's known hazards in my head. I know even shallow, fast-moving water can be strong enough to knock someone over and that, as a nonswimmer, if I fall over, I'm particularly done for. Not to mention I'm still not seeing straight.

I stand there for another moment, arguing with myself, and then I turn and hurry back toward the hotel. I need to get inside and dry, so I can think.

Shaking off the spots in my eyes, I jackknife my way back in through the window, the sash falling closed behind me. I slump against the wall, catching my breath, swiping my hair out of my face. The noise of the wind is instantly muffled.

I turn and press my face against the glass, wondering if I should try again. I can see just the outline of the electric fence beyond the bridge flapping in the wind. It occurs to me that crawling under it in these wet, windy conditions could mean getting electrocuted. And that would be if I could get over the bridge. I feel as if, suddenly, I'm in an enchanted, impassable castle.

My head is throbbing hard enough it makes a zinging in my ears.

I pull out my cell phone. The battery is half down, and I have no way to charge it. I swallow hard and tap my dad's number and wait for the ringtone, knowing it won't come. I try again, and again. I tap the phone lightly with my forehead in frustration. I walk around the room, up and down the stairs, and try every floor for a signal, knowing I won't find it.

I sit for a moment, catching my breath, shivering and sick with worry. I peel out of my wet sweatshirt and use the velvet curtain dangling beside me to dry myself off as best I can. I listen to the howling of the wind.

I think of what my family and my town already think of me. With this in the mix, when I get home, I'll be below rock bottom.

For a long time, I go back and forth. There are no good choices. I know the storm must be passing its closest, and so it should be gone by morning. And I've got a headache that's almost blinding now. Plus, there's still a chance that, if I try every nook and cranny in the hotel, I'll eventually find a signal to call home.

That's ultimately what I decide to do.

The rest of the night stretches ahead of me like some strange kind of dream. I'm wide awake. I look around helplessly, with hours ahead of me and nowhere to go. For now the Rose Hotel belongs to me and I belong to it.

If I were to check the news, I would make a different choice. I would cross the bridge. But it'll be several hours before I find a way to get news of the world beyond the property, and when I do, it will be too late.

I get back to searching for what Elias left me.

What else can I do?

Chapter 19

I'M ON MY KNEES IN ROOM 314, LOOKING through a chest of drawers, when I glance up and happen to see the night lightening outside. I've been so absorbed in what I've been doing I hadn't noticed. I wonder if the demolition crews will even come in the wet weather, and know I should be gone from here when they do. I feel a pang of hunger.

It's rained steadily all night, the kind of rain that sounds like it wants to break the roof. Now that there's enough light to see, I go back to the Van Dorens' and climb upstairs to the Crow's Nest, hoping I can get a good glimpse of the bridge to make sure the water has gone down. My feet are heavy as I climb the stairs. I don't want to face what's waiting for me at home.

What I see from the window makes my stomach do a small, anxious somersault. Things have gotten worse, not better, overnight. The wind is steady and hard, the trees swaying wildly. The sky is a heavy slate gray of fast-moving clouds, the color of a hailstorm I saw once when I was little: a luminous kind of darkness that promises *something coming*. It feels like the world is sucking in its breath.

Also, Main Street is empty: the streets have been almost completely cleared of cars. It's this that causes the first tingle of true fear in me. The emptiness is *wrong*. Finally, almost out of sight but just at the edge of my view to the left, I see the bridge. It's submerged up to the lower rails now.

I pull out my phone and turn it on. Still no signal and my battery is a thin blade of red. I turn it off again.

I stand at the window for several minutes, wondering what to do. I'm picking at the caulk along the windowsill nervously, thinking, when I remember *Stan's radio*.

Where did we leave it?

I hurry down the stairs and look behind the concierge desk. It's there, looking ancient and definitely not like a thing that could possibly work. I take the handle from the back and crank it . . . five times, twenty times, I don't know how many times I should do it. And then I flick the switch.

Sound flickers to life, just fuzz. I toggle the dial from top to bottom, but all I get is static. Sitting there listening, I go back and forth, back and forth with the dial. And then I remember how my dad has an AM station that he turns to when we're stuck in traffic.

I switch to AM and twirl the dial slowly. I find only fuzz, and then a radio announcer talking gently about the velvety voice of Frank Sinatra. I keep scrolling.

Finally, I land on a robotic announcement that's the same kind my dad listens to in the car. I've come to it halfway through a report, so I don't really understand what I'm hearing, but my stomach begins to throb as I catch words about storm winds, and surges, and landfall. I stay like this for several minutes, waiting for something intelligible to surface, and then comes the beep of the broadcast about to begin again. The report circles back through the basics, but they're fuzzy:

"Hurricane Kirk . . . wind gusts up to one hundred fifty miles per hour and expected to worsen . . . storm surges . . . category five . . . . brunt on Manhattan . . ."

And then come numbers and words that mean nothing to me.

I try for more stations, to get a better sense of what and why, but this is the only station I can get besides the Frank Sinatra one. It offers tiny slices of facts but no context. How is the hurricane suddenly heading for northern New Jersey? What exactly does category five mean? I don't understand why things were fine and now they're not.

I guess my crank power must run out fast, because the radio dies. I crank it again, get nothing again but fuzz and "I Did It My Way," and then I just stare out at the whipping trees. I guess the demolishers won't be coming today. And then a thought comes to me: What if Father James has been right all along, and God *is* his personal gangster, and He's sending this storm to punish me after all?

I think about Gabe and Thea and my dad and the nuns. Are they okay? Are we in the evacuation zone? Is that why all the cars from Main Street are gone? Are *they* gone?

I try to talk myself out of my growing worry. I'm in a bedrock monolith four stories high that, according to the brochure, has been here since 1897. My family, if they're told to, will evacuate . . . or already have. The hurricane is named *Kirk*, and surely if it was going to be deadly, the meteorologists would have named it something else.

There's no other choice but to stay. I'll have to shelter here. Wait it out. Leave after the storm or whatever edges of it are headed our way. But what will that look like, and how bad will it be?

It's an eerie day, fear and quiet and the beauty of the hotel mixed together. I try to do the things you hear you should in possible disasters. I go to fill one of the guest room tubs with water before realizing nothing comes out of the tap, given that nobody's paid the water bill since I was eleven. I hang a white sheet out a window facing town like a flag, hoping someone might look across the river and see it and come for me. I hunt for food and water. In the cabinet of the Van Dorens' kitchen, way in the back and probably a thousand years old, I find three cans of bean salad, a can of crushed tomatoes, and a six-pack of Evians plus two lemon San Pellegrinos. I wonder if previous caretakers, or intruders like me, have eaten all the rest. In another drawer, I find a can opener. I devour one of the cans of beans immediately and save the rest. I put a bucket out on one of the windowsills to catch rain just in case. The front of me gets drenched in the three seconds I take to do it.

I look out at the river, a brown blur just at the edge of the rocky bank, where yesterday it was several feet below.

Outside, surreally, a guy paddles past in a kayak in the rain. I yell out the window, trying to get his attention, but then he's gone—already too far away for me to even hope to grab his attention. By the time he vanishes around a bend it already feels like I imagined him.

I return to the radio throughout the day but keep hearing virtually the same report from this morning over and over again. Each time I get a little bit more, an update on location of landfall and speed, but not enough to understand what it means for me.

Finally, I run out of things to keep me busy. And so I turn back to why I came; I have too much time on my hands not to. Fidgeting, wired, the rumble of thunder occasionally rattling far away, I search for Elias's note like one of those brooms in *Fantasia* the sorcerer enchants. I sit combing the past in my mind: the nights we came here, the day at the waterfall, the KISS tree, thinking of *our secrets*. I turn my attention back to the guest rooms, checking each one thoroughly. I leave all the doors open and unlocked, which feels pleasantly rebellious in a way only a rule follower could relish.

The time seems to go slowly, but then not. When you're an insomniac, sometimes you lose hours without noticing, and other times, five minutes stretch on forever. I doze on my feet and wonder about Stan the concierge to distract myself from my growing hunger. He definitely has a mustache and likes to eat hoagies, that's a given. I imagine he has a brother named Mike, who lives next door, and a dog called something like Butch. I hope he's okay. As the day wears on, and my hunger becomes harder to ignore, I'm more and more angry at Elias for his stupid hidden piece of paper. For his whims and his silliness, his games and ghosts.

As evening falls, the weather is about the same as it was in the morning: windy, impassable, but steady. I take this as a good sign that maybe this is the worst it will get. But beyond the windows, I get the feeling that what I know— and what everyone out there knows—is different.

I settle into the Crow's Nest again that night for no other reason than I like having the view of what's coming. I try to self-diagnose my headache and whether it's a concussion, while having no medical skills whatsoever. I flick the button on my cell phone, but it doesn't come on. The battery has run out at last.

It's now, for the first time, that I think of the dam. It's too dark to see any sign of it peeking above the hills. I turn my mind to other things almost immediately, but it stays in the back of my mind, a prickle of warning I want to dismiss.

By the time the dim light limps toward evening, the rain is coming harder, but I'm feeling secure. It's my second night here, and after the storm, no matter how bad it gets, I will make my way home. It's not going to be that bad, I decide.

I crank the radio one last time for good measure. This time, Frank Sinatra is fuzzy, but miraculously, the robot station is clear as a bell.

"Hurricane Kirk has been upgraded to a historic category six, turning its full brunt onto Manhattan and the New Jersey coast after taking a turn at around midnight last night. Gusts in the area will reach their height around nine p.m. tomorrow. Dangerous storm surges, waves, and intense flooding of catastrophic severity are expected. Officials at the National Weather Service are now calling this the fiercest Atlantic storm on record, and those under evacuation orders are now urged to shelter in place."

The report goes on specifically to New York City. There's a listing of bridges and tunnels and subway routes that have been closed until further notice.

There's more, but the station starts to fuzz again and then goes blank.

I sit staring at the radio, disturbed, thinking about the city. How do you get eight million people off an island at the same time? My blood surges under my skin with hot, sudden fear. I try to get my head around it, and how fast things are moving from okay to . . . not okay.

I take in the landscape outside. Green Valley is about twenty miles inland; we may or may not be okay. I'm looking at Chimney Rise and thinking, if there were one place to be safe, if the river were to really overflow, it would be there, high above everything. If shit really hits the fan, that's where I'll go.

In town, I can see a few hardy souls moving inside the windows of the old brick buildings downtown. Maybe they don't think the storm will be that bad. Or maybe they're just helpless; maybe they don't have cars, or they're staying to be with their pets. They must be feeling the same way I do right now: a little out-of-body as we realize we are, each of us, in danger. I feel a lonely ache for home. I want to turn away from it.

Then I see a shape, in one of the buildings, standing as if it's seeing me across the river. I can just make out the splotch of a pale face, jet-black hair, a bright pink shirt. I wave to her. She stands there for a long moment, then waves back. And then she moves deeper into her house and is gone.

Outside, a snake of electricity crackles its way across the river, static weaving through the air, startling me.

I realize that people might die tomorrow. Possibly a lot of people. It feels like the beginning of a nightmare.

I remember my dad telling me once about the eyewalls of hurricanes. They're apparently the thing to watch: the circle of the most violent winds that surround the quiet eye of a spiraling storm, a kind of tower of clouds shot through with thunder and lightning. You only have to make it through the vicious ring of an eyewall—into the eye of the storm and out again—before things begin to get calmer.

I suppose that means this time tomorrow night, that's where Green Valley will be. And I wish I could be somewhere with my family before then. More than that, I wish them far away from it. I stay by the radio for a long time. It keeps me moored to the world in small staticky bursts, but it's a one-way street: the world reaches me but I can't reach it.

In the dark I try to envision the vastness of the storm swirling itself out beyond the coast. I feel a lonely ache for home, for Gabe, his sweetness, his morning breath. I wish I could tell him we are going to be fine. He might pretend to believe me. It might even be true. I find, when I check it, my bucket to catch rain has tipped and fallen off the windowsill. I could eat one whole pizza at least.

Again, electricity snakes across the water. And then, beyond the windows, the shapes of the people I've been watching disappear. Downtown Green Valley flickers and goes dark. The power in town snuffs out like a flame.

Chapter 20

SOMETIME IN THE NIGHT, I MOVE DOWN TO the lobby and curl up near the double doors, instinctively wanting to be closer to escape.

I half dream about New York: the subway underwater, the train tunnels that lead to Manhattan flooded, the stacks under the New York Public Library submerged like Atlantis. I see a ghoulish man shaking his head at me as he takes an elevator downward into clear blue water. I almost think he's real, but I manage to pull myself back.

I wake to wetness.

I shoot up in disbelief, water sloshing my side where

I've slept, and look around in shock. It's morning. Water is pooling and lapping into the lobby from under the entrance doors.

From here, through the window, I can see the field is submerged, its surface hidden under shin-deep water in motion. The river has breached its banks and spilled across and swallowed the grass.

I know that if the field looks this way, downtown, which is lower, must be inundated. I hurry up to the Crow's Nest to see.

I forget to breathe.

From above, the river is no longer a river but a brown blur engulfing the lowlands of our valley. Main Street is underwater, just like the fields around the hotel. I look for the dam, knowing that if the river is this high it must be nearly overflowing. But of course, in the rain I can't see it at all.

Outside, there are birds crossing the sky again. Maybe two or three hundred of them. But do birds generally fly in the rain, much less *flock* in it?

"No," I say out loud. And startle myself with the sound of my own voice.

I crank the radio, afraid of what I'll hear, but the truth

is, I hear nothing. The station has completely gone out. I toss the radio on the floor and kick it, a guttural sound escaping me.

The hotel gives a creak somewhere deep below in its foundations, and then a groan. I stop for a minute to listen, but the sound disappears.

I find I'm scared enough to feel nauseous. High as I can climb above it, the wetness of the lobby is something I wouldn't have imagined. It feels now like no matter how high I go, no matter how many rooms I have to hide in, the Rose is no impenetrable fortress after all. I'm just in a building, and buildings can fill up with water; they can even come down. All sorts of things can happen.

I open the window, letting the wind blow in.

"I give up!" I yell out into the air. "I give up, Elias! Fuck your piece of paper!"

I yell some more swear words up toward the clouds for good measure.

Even as I do this, I hear it: the wind getting louder. I slam the window shut against it.

It'll climb, the wind . . . if the reports are to be believed. Until tonight, around 9:00.

I have no idea how bad it will get before then.

—✳—

All morning and early afternoon, as the weather gets fiercer and louder, building toward whatever it's building to . . . I try to think about anything but my growing fear and the hunger that gnaws me. For now I resist eating what meager food I have. I wish I had a way to watch the news. I miss the endless supply of commentary that makes you feel like you're experiencing something big with other people even when you're alone.

But since I have nothing of the sort, I do headstands. I sing to myself. I dance. I kick antiques from one end of the lobby to the other and yell every dirty word I can think of down all the hallways. In one of the guest room bathrooms I use my hands to squeeze my face into funny shapes, and study my pupils to see if I'm still concussed (seems to me I am, given that my head still hurts and my ears still ring). I write things on the hotel walls with markers I find in a guest room drawer. I drink two bottles of water and eventually, my willpower evaporating, eat the last two cans of beans.

Also, and stranger, I keep thinking I hear noises in the hotel: taps, steps, even a howl. But that's what happens in an old hotel; even the oldest ghost story in the world will tell you that. I know it's the wind creating updrafts, rattling windows and doors.

The trees across the field are whipping so hard they're almost sideways, and the promised winds are still hours away. The water continues to spill in, though it rises slowly. It's the building itself that scares me, and the creaks I hear every now and then coming from far below. I feel them in my feet.

How much harder can winds blow before buildings start to break?

By late afternoon, it looks and feels like night. Outside, the waterlogged fields are full of churning debris: trash cans, tires, a couch, a street sign. I can see the thunderstorms approaching, lightning flickering in the gray, low sky. The thunder rumbles so loudly it makes the floor beneath me vibrate. I know I should move deeper into the hotel and away from the glass windows, but it's hard to look away.

An hour passes, maybe two. The emptiness in my stomach has taken on a panicked edge, and I feel disheveled, grimy, strange to myself. Tree limbs tumble across the grounds, one of them landing tangled in the round stone fountain in what used to be the courtyard. The main doors thump as if they'll be blown open. Upstairs, I hear glass shatter in one of the guest rooms.

I am sitting in the hallway in the mezzanine, with my back to the wall, facing out onto the lobby, defunct radio in my lap, when the thing suddenly blares on.

On reflex, I drop it.

I stare at it like a monster come to life. The gentle radio host is back.

I look around, wondering if somehow the wind, the electricity, the barometric pressure could have turned it back on. Maybe the crank was stuck and unstuck itself. Still, the hairs on my neck stand up.

In any case, I reach for it and turn the dials, only to find the other station is still out. I give the radio the middle finger a few times and let out another guttural yell. And finally, I give up, and give in. I turn back to Frank Sinatra.

I know I should flick the radio off, but I can't bring myself to do it: it's just so nice to hear another voice.

And then the DJ says he has something especially appropriate for tonight's weather, going out to all the people of New York City, and after a temporary lag, a song comes on called "Summer Wind."

It's such a weird thing to play in the face of disaster, I

almost feel like it can't be real. The DJ has a sick sense of humor, or maybe he's just making the best of a bad situation. Or maybe I'm dreaming it.

In any case, I like the song. I sit listening to Sinatra's voice drift through the dimness . . . echoey and otherworldly in how connected it feels to the storm and the room and the night.

The summer wind came blowin' in from across the sea
It lingered there to touch your hair and walk with me . . .

Does the world have its eyes on us right now? Are people everywhere watching to see what this storm will do, or are we a cartoon place to them, just as places like Australia and Bangladesh once were to me? I try to doze off, but I also try not to *try*, because trying is the surest way to startle away anything you want most.

Somewhere far below, I hear another window break, and I shudder. It's followed by the sound of more things breaking in response—maybe a vase blown over, maybe some dishes at Tipper's.

I see something out on the river, a car floating down it. It looks like there might be someone inside, and I feel a tremor of nausea at the thought, but I hope it's just a trick of the light.

Through the window, I catch glimpses of the stone angels at the corners of the roof and beyond them, the wide roiling sky, churning like pale sheets pulled back across a bed. The rain is still pummeling the roof, the windows, the walls. My eyes travel up to the main entrance, to the carvings and ornate marble sconces. And a tickle begins at the back of my neck.

Like with most revelations, I'm not thinking of what I've been looking for when I discover it. It comes to me when my mind is somewhere else.

Chapter 21

MY EYES HAVE BEEN ON THE STATUE FOR A long time. But in the dim evening light, I haven't really *seen* it. From the mezzanine I'm almost level with it, since it graces the space above the double doors, and the doors are so tall they end only inches below the second floor.

I've walked under this statue a million times, but I've never taken a close look. Elias, on the other hand: he was always looking up.

I'm not sure which angel she's supposed to be: temperance or patience or faith, or whatever else. But now I see the similarities immediately: arms outstretched, face concerned, noble, kind. She's so much like the guardian angel in my charm bracelet; the one I wore when I was a kid, the one who guarded clueless children crossing streams.

And I think suddenly of what Elias said about her the day we met, when I dangled my bracelet in front of him, before we became brother and sister by swapping blood.

She looks like she's hiding something.

I feel an itch of recognition, cold certainty crawling all over my body. It's like the statue version of a pun: to *hide* something in the hands of an angel who *looks like she's hiding something.* Also, it's magical—a supernatural being watching over us. It's all of Elias's favorite things. I study the wide ledge that leads to the statue.

He *wouldn't.* He *couldn't.*

But. A white ledge runs along the wall at the level of my feet, a sort of lip of wood that overhangs the space below to frame it. And there's another, narrower, decorative bar—like a rail-shaped molding—along the wall at shoulder height. He might have hung on to it while standing on the ledge. For someone who was unafraid of falling, it would have been simple enough. And Elias knew I could climb.

And then I see the dust along the ledge, so thick stepping on it would have been like leaving fossils. There's the mark of the tip of a big sneaker.

I'm trembling, and *of course* he would put it somewhere I'd be scared to go.

It's only about fifteen steps to reach it. But the steps could kill me. I gaze down at the flooded lobby below.

Hands shaking, I hitch my leg over the mezzanine rail, sliding carefully to stand on the other side of it, heels suspended above the lobby as I cling tight. I grasp the bar with one hand, then the other, and sidestep my way slowly along the ledge, not looking down. My hands are shaking so hard I worry I will lose my grasp, but I am both terrified and strong.

Soon I'm at the corner. I slide the last few feet that remain, dust falling in tufts around my feet to the wet expanse below.

I reach the angel, and carefully, taking several moments to cement my balance, I slide one hand along her cold stone cheek to her collarbone, feeling my way with my trembling fingers along the crevices.

I find it clasped in her left hand, nestled in the gap made by her flexed stone fingers: I feel the corner of it first, a small, crisply folded square. I stop shaking, but I also stop breathing. I forget everything: storm, building, flood.

I grasp the paper carefully with my thumb and forefinger, but as I pull it out, it snags in the crack between the angel's fingers and for a moment I feel it slip toward the emptiness below. I pinch it with my nails, just at the edge, and pull it close to me.

The shaking returns as I cup it against me, a folded square the size of a stamp. I tuck it in my shirt at the top of my bra, and then slide back along the ledge in reverse, still clasping the shoulder-height bar with numb fingers.

By the time I get to the mezzanine, my legs are jelly, my face and side smudged with wet fuzz and dust, my hair matted, my head pounding. I hoist myself over and onto the floor, lying on my back, breathing, safe.

And then I sit up and pull the paper back out of my shirt.

I hesitate. I find I can't bring myself to open it yet. This might be the last most exciting thing to happen to me, if I don't make it out of here. These might be the last words from Elias I will ever get.

There is a sadness with getting what you want, mixed with all the fear. Because what do you do with yourself after you get it?

I stand and walk down the hall to room 203 and sit

down gently on the end of the bed. I look at myself in the mirror: straggly, pale, exhausted.

I stare down at the paper in my hand and open it.

It's not words, after all.

20°46'16.5" S, 115°20'58.1" E

My heart gives a lurch.

I stare at it for several moments, thinking there's some mistake—it's not the right piece of paper, or maybe all along Elias was messing with me. And then, of course, I realize.

I hear Elias in the mausoleum in the rain telling me about the place, trying to lull me to sleep. The spot where he was going to make a stand against the sinking of the world. It's as mythical to me as Saint Eia's relic, and yet here it is in numbers: Elias's precious beach, real and find-able. Still out there and maybe not too late to walk across. Maybe not swallowed up yet by the sea. I repeat the numbers to myself again and again like a spell, or a wish, or a prayer.

I feel my shoulders shake and I am crying. For Elias's beach and how I will never see it. For the Gabes and Barneys I wish I could save that beach for. And because I am afraid. Not just of hurricanes but of *all the things*.

Upstairs, I hear more glass shatter. Somewhere a tree has broken a window.

I lie down on the bed and think of Elias's body wrapped around mine.

I pull the paper close to my chest and curl around it. I listen to the hotel creak and groan beneath me like a sinking ship.

Minutes later, some deep worrisome thing rouses me. It's a noise, though also . . . not really a noise. I feel it in my body, like the distant rattle of an earthquake. I read once that when Krakatoa erupted, you could hear it three thousand miles away. It feels like that.

Then the next minute, I'm in utter silence. I try to grasp how absolutely still and calm it all is, but it's almost too shocking to fathom.

And I realize that, while I've been busy solving Elias's mystery, we've gotten through the eyewall. We are in the eye of the storm.

Chapter 22

I WALK TO THE WINDOW. THE CLOUDS HAVE parted around a circle of bright night; the moon shines overhead, and the stars are out. It feels like a stillness you can't shake or find your way out of—so peaceful, so clear—like the sky's been washed clean. I stare up in wonder, stunned by the abnormal calm.

Far below I can hear the water sloshing gently on the first floor.

The paper is still curled into my hand. I fold it tightly and tuck it into my coin pocket.

I'm standing in the space of time it takes for water to travel, but I don't know it yet.

If it weren't for the quiet, I wouldn't hear it.

It's a slapping, slippery sound, confusing because sounds like *that* are usually soft. This one is loud. It's halfway between a slap and a *boom*.

I stand cocking my head, listening, thinking maybe I've imagined it. I'm just turning my attention back to the moon when I hear it again, coming from below.

Slap. Boom.

I walk into the hall and peer down into the lobby— illuminated with moonlight but with nothing amiss except the slow trickle of water sloshing along the floor. I pad down the grand stairs, peering around in the glowing dimness.

Slap. Boom. On instinct, my legs begin to shake.

I come to the bottom of the stairs and stand there squinting, bewildered. I don't want to get closer to the sound, but it might be worse not to know what it is. Finally, I wade into the water of the lobby, which reaches just up to my ankles.

Here on ground level, it's easier to determine that the pounding's coming from the side of the hotel that faces the river. I walk slowly in that direction, trying to make sense of what I see: something is moving outside the glass so strangely in the night, high up against the glass, taller than me. It's a shadow that doesn't end but keeps swaying back and forth . . . as if the line of the earth is tilting. *Slap. Boom.*

And then I see it for what it is: the shadow is a wall of water. It's like a reverse aquarium, with water pressing at the walls. It sways against the doors, then retreats. *Slap. Boom*: it sways again. A thin trickle is pouring through the crack between the doors, all the way from the top. I watch, paralyzed.

I know it all at once: the distant quaking that rattled my body like Krakatoa, the water at the doors. I know what's happened. The dam. The dam has burst.

Slap. Boom. Cracks snake their way in all directions along the glass, and with another slap of water comes the deafening sound of shattering.

I'm across the lobby from the grand stairs. I start toward them but not as fast as water can move. I'm halfway across when the waves crash around me, and I lose my footing.

I'm swiped forward and sideways. In the dark my hands slam against a table that's flipped up against me and then I'm moving along, carried by a current that throws me like a rag. I slam with force into a corner, but I don't know which one or where it is.

And then I see I'm being washed toward a window, and just as I reach it, I snag on a corner of the sill. I feel glass scrape my side, but I cling onto the sill with both hands, and the current shifts for a moment as I fall back and somehow find my footing.

For a moment I'm on hands and knees and half underwater, and then I'm up and sloshing onto the stairs, water up to my waist as I lunge for the banister and pull myself up and over the rail.

I fall limp for a moment and then scramble up the steps, turning to look only when I'm at the top, sucking in breath and clutching my side, which bleeds from a web of shallow cuts.

I am shaking, shaking, shaking so hard my teeth clack against each other. My vision goes in and out, like curtains closing and opening again.

My bones ache. My teeth chatter as I stare down in shock at the wreckage of the lobby. The tables, the vases, the chairs are floating out through the shattered space where the windows were. I could swear I see the walls shake.

Outside, the storm is whipping itself into a frenzy again as we plunge out of the eye.

And then I see something across the river that turns my panic to something like terror.

Across the gorge, the house with the bright blue shutters begins to *move*. Five, ten, twenty seconds it wobbles and then slips into the water as smoothly as a swimmer, its roof bobbing as it's swallowed by the rapids. I watch an entire house . . . *float away*. And then comes a shudder underneath me for certain this time. The hotel—all four floors and monolithic stone ceiling and eighty-five guest rooms of it—is *moving* too.

And I can't swim.

I can't swim.

I can't swim.

Chapter 23

I CLIMB THE FLIGHTS OF STAIRS, WANTING to be as far from the ground as possible. Legs aching, I wind up at the Crow's Nest again. It's almost dawn, and the floor rattles every now and then beneath me. Beyond the window, at the base of Cub Mountain, Main Street is now a river.

Stunned, I watch dusty wardrobes, clocks, cabinets, dressers, and yellowed books float out of the Rose and into the rushing expanse outside. I watch another house along the gorge tumble into the river. There can't be anyone in it, I think. I try to believe it.

How fast can a river rise? How fast can water swallow a cliff?

My mind seems to float somewhere above my body, and I think, This is what being out of body is. It's your mind trying to save itself by imagining itself *out, up, away.* There's too much to fear. Not to mention the shaking hands, the heart trying to pound its way out of the ribs.

I frantically need to undo being here, un-climb through the window, un-ride my bike to the bridge, un-find Elias that first night he was hunting ghosts, un-meet him the day I climbed the KISS tree. I need to go back and turn left instead of right. In my dazed state, I can almost envision it. I close my eyes and make promises to nobody I believe in. If you get me out of here I'll be braver. I'll pray sometimes. I'll do whatever rituals God requires.

The building sways and settles back in again, like it's reluctant to go. But I see, through the window, that a corner of it has already left: over near the west entrance, a hunk of wall and floor has been ripped away.

I don't know how long I stand there. My head swims and everything is hazy. I'm sleepless, concussed, hungry, and I am sure I'm going to die. It could be five minutes, it could be an hour that passes as I watch the water engulf my safe pocket of the world. I stare out at Chimney Rise, its overlook far above the water. It's too late to reach it now.

I'm thinking of things I like about living more than I realized; insane things considering how trivial they are. I like Burger King fries. I like watching my dad listening to Hall & Oates. The smell of new tennis balls. I love this old collection of unicorn stickers I have in a cookie tin in my closet. Maybe this is life flashing before your eyes: maybe it's supposed to be mundane.

The groaning underneath the hotel is almost constant. The building is talking to me like it's telling me it's too old for this shit. From my high perch, I listen for the slide of bricks and the sound of floors breaking apart.

And then, something happens that I do not expect.

I hear someone singing.

It turns out I am not alone.

Chapter 24

IS IT POSSIBLE FOR BLOOD TO FREEZE? MY pulse feels like it pauses.

I stand, and wait, and listen as the singing goes silent. But then it starts again, louder than before, a woman's voice.

Am I imagining it, or is she singing a song I know from the Frank Sinatra channel? "Fly Me to the Moon."

I walk down the stairs again and back out to the mezzanine. I am no longer shaking.

Someone in a white sundress is standing about halfway down the grand stairs. She's not looking at me but out the windows that have been ripped into holes.

It is as if everything—the crumbling hotel, the water—goes on mute around me, fading into background noise. I am not myself. I am exhausted and empty, starved and at the end of myself. But I know from the photos, from her clothes, from her face, who she is.

"Mrs. . . . Van Doren?" I ask.

The singing stops abruptly. She glances up at me, as if she's not at all surprised to see me. Dark circles lie under her eyes.

"We'll have to leave soon," she says, her voice echoing against water and walls. "This place will not hold."

I stand frozen. I'm trying to make sense of lots of things at once. One, that she's here, that anyone is here. Two, who she *is*. My head swims.

"I thought you were dead," I say stupidly.

She meets my gaze and shakes her head.

"Not dead," she says. "Just hiding."

I blink at her for several seconds. She glances down at the ruins of what's happening below. I think about the strange aura of the residence, the way it feels lived-in even now. The hidden key.

"Why?" I sputter. It's all I can think to say.

She glances up at me again. "My family died," she answers, as if it's obvious. As if such a loss could explain any of the surreal and nonsensical things a person might do.

I'm so numb, so floaty. It's uncanny but not necessarily impossible. She could have survived the crash. Had someone running her errands, bringing her groceries. Rich people can pay anyone to do anything.

"You didn't call the cops on us," I say.

She gazes at me, unreadable, and then out the window again.

"Things aren't looking good in Manhattan, you know. I'm afraid for them."

"I know," I say.

"Then again," she goes on, "who are we to talk?" This time, her mouth crooks bitterly and she swallows, hard. "We're in trouble, aren't we?" She looks down the hall again, the one that leads to the pool. "I'd say it's time to evacuate." Her posture stiffens. "Have to go underwater, through the pool area, to get up to Chimney Rise. It'll be hard, but if we can swim to the bottom of those stairs on the other side, I'd say we have a twenty percent chance of making it."

It hits me like a punch. That she's going to leave me.

"I have a *zero* percent chance," I say. "I can't swim."

She startles for a moment, surprised. She turns again to contemplate the churning water below, sweeping away all in its path. The hall to the pool area is three-quarters full and completely submerged below the stairs, but it's clear she's truly going to do it. Even though I can't believe she would. "The only way out is through."

I shake my head. I'm thinking, you can't just suddenly know how to swim.

"I . . . have to stay," I say. For a moment, Mrs. Van Doren seems to flicker, or rather my eyesight does.

"And wait for the place to collapse?" she asks.

I try to get my eyes to focus. My center wobbles. I know she's right. Collapse is coming. A building can't stand when the things that hold it up are torn away.

Mrs. Van Doren gives me a sympathetic smile. "I'm not saying I don't understand you. You can breathe in here at least, but once you leave . . ." She gestures out to the hallway, toward the submerged pool room, and trails off. "Still, you've got to make a go of it, at least."

I shake my head furiously. I feel I might be sick.

She moves up the stairs a step or two, as if to reach for my hand to give me encouragement. But something holds her back. And I feel more and more the strangeness of her, the way she moves weightlessly on the stairs.

"I'm a cautious fish," I breathe, near tears.

She leans on the railing, again somehow weightlessly.

I gaze at her, adding up her explanations, her sundress the same one from her photo in the Crow's Nest. I'm starting to think things through. I'm concussed, eternally sleep-deprived, and losing my mind. I once saw a zebra where a zebra rug should be.

"You're a ghost," I say, leveling it at her. My skin crawls hot and cold.

She doesn't say anything. Which seems like a yes. I shudder.

"Elias was looking for you," I whisper, even though I know she's not really there. I know she's a ghost I'm *imagining*: a figment of my imagination *pretending* to be a ghost *pretending* to be a person.

"Look. Cassie, I'm sorry about all of it. The world is full of terrors; there's no way around it. There's nothing more foolish than taking that on. But you have to decide whether to be foolish." She pauses, flinching as the railing beside us shudders. "Weirder things have happened," she goes on, "than that it turns out there's something to believe in anyway."

She looks at me, then stiffens up her shoulders, as if she's encouraging me at the outset of a soccer game. "I, for one, think we can make it."

She moves a step down, into the water, lowering herself

slowly until it comes up to her waist.

"You'll die!" I yell. I leap down two stairs at a time to grab her. I know now she's not real. But I'm afraid for her anyway.

Still, the rushing water doesn't appear to tug at her. She moves toward the hall that leads down, down, down. She's already half submerged and pulling herself deeper, until only her head is above water.

"You were never here," I say finally.

She stares back at me, expressionless.

A moment later, she sinks underwater. I rush up to see what's become of her, but she's nowhere in sight. And just like that, as fast as she's appeared, Mrs. Van Doren is gone.

Chapter 25

I'M SITTING AT THE TOP OF THE STAIRS, IN A spot that hasn't been reached by the water yet, but it will be. The river is climbing fast.

A handful of bricks have fallen from the ceiling, making holes for the rain to come through. What used to be the entrance doors are now an open gash.

I am watching it all come down, breathing fast. The hallway that leads to the pool room that leads to Chimney Rise is almost completely underwater now. I think about that moment before people dive into cold pools, the first leap after long winters.

How do you pick your moment? When you have minutes left to give something up, every second takes on a preciousness. So how do you say . . . *now* I go? When you might get ten minutes more?

I think about what Elias said about swimming: you just create momentum with your limbs. And I know it doesn't matter what he said; I still can't swim. But I do have a choice. I can go all the way up to the Crow's Nest, sit by the window, watch the world, and wait for the collapse . . . stretch out my time to live for a little bit longer. Or I can lower myself into the water and try to make it out. Only one of my choices has hope in it.

In the end, it is Gabe who decides it.

It's Gabe I have a 1 percent chance of making it back to.

I try to *will* my feet to step down into the water, but I'm frozen to the spot. My breath is my new best friend; I've never for a second considered what it'd be like not to have it. And now I may be gulping my last. I find I'm hyperventilating.

I take a step. One foot then the other, breath ragged, hands shaking, white-knuckling the handrail. The stairs still hold; they have not crumbled away under the current.

For as long as possible, I will pull myself along.

Another wide decorative rail runs along the wall and I reach for that, trying to wrap my fingers around it as I step down farther into the water that tugs at my feet, my ankles, my knees as I get lower in. Still I manage to stay upright as I slide and stumble and push forward. I don't even feel the cold, I'm so cold already.

I glide along the wall, pushed hard against it, but at least I'm pushed in the right direction. My chest is smushed, but I'm breathing. I'm terrified my numb hands will let the railing go. I know that without it, I'm lost.

Finally, I get to the edge of the hall that leads down to the pool. If I'm to go down, I have to go under. I know the exit door is one flight below, across the room, and the current might push enough to get me there. My breath has taken off without me; my whole body shudders violently. How am I supposed to catch a breath I can't hold? My pulse throbs everywhere: my feet, my head, my gut. Animal instincts tell me to turn back, *demand* that I do.

I'm petrified now, because I *can't* go back. There's no way to fight back to the stairs against the current. If I try and fail, I'll lose any strength I have for what's below. There's only down. Panicked, my body fights me. I look up at the ceiling as if it's my favorite thing in the world and I need to say goodbye to it.

I try to think of as many things I love as I can. Chipmunks. Musty rooms. Gabe's cheeks when he was a baby. My dad drinking coffee. Elias pointing out the North Star once, two warm bodies in the woods.

I try to calm myself to settle my heartbeat and my breathing. I take deep, slow breaths despite the pounding of my blood.

I bob another moment on the water's surface before I think about Gabe one more time for courage and force the impossible: the small twitch of my fingers that lets the rails go. I suck in a deep breath—as deep as I can stand and maybe the last—and I'm under.

I'm not a person anymore; I'm an animal, a blankness with no thoughts but *survive*. The water is darkness. I kick my way down, pulling along crevices and cracks in the walls, and my hands find the stair rail. I kick too hard as my hands claw at it, pulling myself along, yanking so hard it feels I will lose my arms. My lungs start to ache too soon. I won't make it to the bottom of the stairs, much less across the pool room to the door.

It feels like forever, but it is maybe thirty seconds. I can't see, and the pressure of my lungs is building.

I yank my way to the end of the rail and then I reach out for something to hold on to to pull me toward the exit, but I am turned around, disoriented; I don't know where it is. This is when I get frantic. I stroke forward but it takes me nowhere.

My lungs scream. The air throbs in my chest.

I don't choose a direction; I only kick wildly forward, lost in empty terror. I flail into a raging current and that's when I lose it. My breath rushes out of me.

Water explodes into my lungs like rocks.

I feel myself swiped forward. In the dark my hands slam against concrete, my shoulder hits a wall so hard my skull rattles, and I'm carried and thrown. I slam into a corner—down or sideways I don't know, but suddenly, somehow, I'm in air. A dark pocket, indoors.

I gasp and I'm pulled under again.

I reach for anything, fingers cracking against surfaces, knees and legs bucking. There's nothing but an instinct to flail, surface, get breath.

Something hits me, moving in the same direction, and I grab it. I hold on to it and try to pull myself above water. The current shifts, just a moment.

I'm yanked down again and then I'm shooting through

and out of something and I'm up. I'm flung into air and breathe for one gasping moment and then go under again. It's long enough to know I am outside.

I'm up in air long enough to see where I've come from: the shattered glass pyramid of the lower roof. Chimney Rise, with its promise of height and safety, is falling far behind me, the river carrying me away from it. But I am breathing. I cling to whatever it is I'm holding. Which turns out to be half a lounger, escaped from the old pool.

I barrel down the river of what used to be the hotel grounds, along with a cluster of a hundred empty soda bottles that have washed out of somewhere. The lounger bobs under me, too light to stabilize and too slippery to keep a grip on. I slam against a floating metal pole. A car sails past and I go under again, yanked by its undertow, surfacing to find it gone.

I'm being spun in a washing machine, but my arms somehow cling to my makeshift buoy.

A tire floats past me—then a whole stampede of tires. Hesitating, I dive for one, hooking an arm over the edge of it as I let the lounger go, my nails jagged from clutching at stone, fingertips bleeding. I can't make my body work, just the arm: I pour all my strength there. With a weak lurch I pull the tire close and cling to it, and groan with hope because it doesn't sink. My legs smack debris underwater.

I clamber farther up onto my tire, and cling, and breathe, and close my eyes. The houses and brick buildings of Green Valley sail past me, then are gone.

And far behind me, just around the curve of the river before it bends, I watch the outline of the Rose Hotel crumble into the gorge, and vanish.

Chapter 26

I SEE STRANGE THINGS AS I AM CARRIED along the Green Valley River.

I see a car floating with a Hawaiian dancer on the dashboard, moving so slowly it looks like it's cruising. I see a pet snake in its aquarium, floating on top of a door. I see a drawer with everything still inside it. Around me floats all the evidence of life in Green Valley and the surrounding towns: books, bags of bread, a backpack, a painting.

My tire moves like a sea-built vessel, sluicing down rapids, gliding around curves in the flow of the water. But I am only half on it, and I don't have the strength to get farther up. I will, I know, let go sometime. Maybe not now, or in the next several minutes, but sometime soon, I will run out of strength. I can only cling as hard as I can and gaze at the known world getting farther and farther away from me.

Soon the river is widening, the shores getting farther instead of closer. I've given up trying to care: you can't wish yourself landward. And I'm tired, so tired and cold. Whatever was left of my beaten-down mind is drifting. I start to see impossible things. A couch that at first appears to be a boat. A cloud in the dim dawn sky that looks like a snake eating an apple.

The shores widen outward, and outward some more, and then, with a whoosh, I am washed out into open water, a clearing between two spits of land, suddenly calm. I think I might be somewhere in the flooded Meadowlands, but if that's the case, I see nothing to orient me—I wouldn't know what to look for, anyway.

And then, circling, I do see something. And catch my breath.

To picture Manhattan in the flood, you have to try to picture it like this: the city up to its knees in water, a back of bristled buildings rising in a river that's joined to the sea.

I lie floating, fighting for my breath, and watch it come into view.

It's morning but not yet light, and even though it seems the city shouldn't have power, the lights of the skyscrapers glitter. Helicopters buzz around the skyline. I see the tiny dots of rescue boats glowing like beacons, dots of what might be people in the water. They are so small under the vast, approaching sky, the city a confluence of a million chaotic things, cobbled together and humming with life. I probably won't live to see what has survived.

"We are so stupid," I say to my tire. I am crying, my face against the rubber. Because I fucking love these idiots who have fucked up the world.

There may come a time when we don't remember what it was like before. How first we said it didn't exist, then that it might exist but it wasn't our fault, and then that it was our fault but we couldn't do anything about it anyway. We might not remember that before the weather was coming for us, we threw a better time away with both hands.

I bob, catching mouthfuls of water, slipping. I could end up at the bottom of the Hudson River like all the gangsters.

I will sleep with the fishes tonight. I want to make a joke about this to someone. The loneliness of knowing that I never will is crushing.

I float on the current and keep my eyes on the lights as if they could prevent me from sinking.

And then the hairs stand up on my neck and my eyelids quiver and I see them, so tiny and distant, up around the spires of the Chrysler Building and soaring above the peak of the Freedom Tower. They flutter in the dying wind, the quieting storm, buffeted by a swirl of clouds so wide they look like they might be battered down out of the sky.

I'm imagining them, of course. I have read about it, in a book called *Supernatural Mysteries, Debunked.* By thinking of them, I've summoned them.

I know it's all in my head. But still, I want so badly to reach them.

I don't believe in them. But the dead have come for me anyway.

Chapter 27

THE COAST GUARD PLUCKS THOUSANDS OF people out of the water in the days following Hurricane Kirk. Many others die.

By the time the boat gets me from the bay, it's nightfall. The other survivors and I look at each other openly, nakedly, as if we are forever tied together by what we suddenly know. We know something that is impossible to say: the fear, and the shattering beauty of life when it almost leaves you.

It's a clear night, and the moon is so bright and *still there* for me to see; I feel like it's the first time I'm seeing it at all. To have my hands on the side of the boat, to smell the river air, to breathe, to wiggle my feet: all of it is stunning. To think of eating a French fry or doing algebra or sitting in the park seems too lovely to be possible. I'm so keenly aware that I'm still me, still this person in this body in this life. And amid the trauma of what's all around me, I glow with it.

Two opposite things can be true at the same time, despite what Father James would say. People are good at destroying and hiding and keeping our egos insulated; we blame and deflect; and every time we feel most right we are at least 20 percent wrong.

We are also good at building. And making do. And changing. And saving. And repairing. We are good at adapting, giving, fixing, apologizing. Forgiving. Well, maybe not forgiving. Maybe I am not yet good at that.

Back home, I feel like Frodo coming back to the Shire: Green Valley is *so* green, so safe, and so small. And also, ill fitting. My birthday comes; I turn eighteen. My family, I learn, sheltered through the storm in Pennsylvania. At first, they don't even ask me what I was doing at the Rose Hotel. It comes out over time.

People are devastated by the floods, and also they want to forget them. We don't pretend the weather isn't changing anymore, but we still fight over what to do. I know we each see something different when we look at the same blue sky. But our town is still green, still safe, still calm, rebuilding. It's just that danger is closer now; fear bites more and more at our edges.

I wish I could say this means that, in the midst of such a real enemy to face, people jump like fleas off Father James. That's not exactly the case. Some cling tighter to him than ever, believe in him and his anger more than ever in the face of so much to fear. If anything, according to him, the hurricane is more than ever a reason to blame everyone else. But fewer people love him than before. His sermons become less well attended.

The parish extends an olive branch to me in the form of asking me to do a reading, a letter from Paul to the Corinthians. While the nuns have never given up on me, the church has let me back in slowly, my near death changing things, I guess. Of course, Father James is the priest presiding.

I clench the pew ahead of me, waiting. When it's time, I stand and walk to the lectern.

I open my Saint Eia book instead of the Bible and read the Bertolt Brecht poem from the foreword. A poem written by a man in another age gone wild.

"'To Those Born Later,'" I say, looking up at the congregation, swallowing. I am still not brave around crowds.

To the cities I came in a time of disorder
That was ruled by hunger.
I sheltered with the people in a time of uproar
And then I joined in their rebellion.
That's how I passed my time that was given to me on this
    Earth.

I ate my dinners between the battles,
I lay down to sleep among the murderers,
I didn't care for much for love
And for nature's beauties I had little patience.
That's how I passed my time that was given to me on this
    Earth.

The city streets all led to foul swamps in my time,
My speech betrayed me to the butchers.
I could do only little

I swallow again.

> *But without me those that ruled could not sleep so easily:*
> *That's what I hoped.*

I pause, look up. Everyone is confused. My hands are shaking, and I am aware I look ridiculously nervous.

> *That's how I passed my time that was given to me on this*
> *Earth.*

> *Our forces were slight and small,*
> *Our goal lay in the far distance*
> *Clearly in our sights,*
> *If for me myself beyond my reaching.*
> *That's how I passed my time that was given to me on this*
> *Earth.*

I look up again when I finish, the rage and bloodlust of the poem pulsing through my veins. But it's comical. Everyone is blinking at me like they don't even know what I said, as if I'd read a letter from Paul to the Corinthians after all.

I close the book. Thea and Gabe and my dad are

watching me from the eighth pew, looking somewhere between horrified and bewildered. And then I look at Father James.

"I'm so damn tired of men like you," I say.

Now they hear me. Amid gasps, and shuffles in the pews, I step back from the podium and into the aisle, and walk out of the church.

They'll think all sorts of things about me: that I'm anti-Catholic or anti-God, that I'm full of hatred. They will read me in any way they want to; you never say things exactly right. But I follow the beat of my pulse out the double doors.

That night I sleep. Every night after, I sleep. I sleep the sleep of people who can fall asleep inside of mausoleums, on floors, in crowded trains . . . the sleep of people who are not two things, but one. I sleep like I am true.

Maybe Green Valley has grown tired too, after all. By December, the powers that be have *Father Jamesed* Father James off to a parish in Yonkers.

Some other monster will come in to replace him, no doubt. These things repeat throughout time.

But I won't be here to see them.

—✳—

The waters recede from Manhattan, and after months, in between classes and school, I volunteer for an online job with the New York Public Library, cataloguing books they lost in the flood. It's a tiny dent, but you've got to start somewhere.

Meanwhile, Thea has changed. She wants to be with Gabe all the time. She dotes on him like the second mother he always needed. A kind of bellwether, she's turned on Father James now that he's gone. Because once it became personal, she didn't need to imagine it.

She promises me that things will be okay with the weather. And I envy her the way she has of believing that what comforts her is true, and I hope that she's right. One night she appears at the threshold of my room but does not come in, only stands in the doorway, watching me. She's been watching me for days like this, bringing me Twizzlers, coffee, her favorite bottles of nail polish with offers to give me a manicure. I was almost dead, after all.

"I just want you to feel the safety of believing," she says. "And I want you to go to heaven."

I put out my hands, open palmed. "It's not like I want to be damned."

I don't tell her the things I saw above the river. She'd be so convinced they were real, while I never will be. But I'm not convinced I imagined them either. As Elias said, it's not really about being certain.

"Believers are like snowflakes, you know," Sister Suzanne says, on a day I am loitering at the convent even though my job there's done. "Don't assume you aren't one just because you doubt everything and tell priests off in church."

By the time Gabe is ready to start first grade—deep into the school year, when his doctor has approved it—he's managing to walk with a pronounced limp. Each step is a little tug on my soul.

Will he get teased? I wonder. Will he ever run as fast as he wants? Will he have a great life? How can I guarantee it?

I drop him off before I drive myself to class, even though Thea or Dad could do it. I'm terrified to watch him go, with his lopsided gait, his fearlessness despite what he's been through. I want to stand by the window of his classroom and watch over him, make sure nothing happens. Does he remember Cheetos can be choking hazards? Someone that small leaves the footprint on your heart of at least three adult humans. Then again, I am describing every kid.

I remember when he was a baby, I could wrap myself around him and know that if anything came for him, I could put my body in front of him to take the blow first.

When he gets home, he tells me something he learned from his friends. He tells me sisters are supposed to have their own lives. He tells me I'm a little bit clingy.

That night I'm in my room, staring at a satellite image online. The paper is mostly obliterated at the folds but it doesn't matter. The coordinates on the paper remain, faded but legible. There are no photos of Elias's beach up close, and it's probably better like that. But from above, it looks like a lip of cream pinned between the dark mouth of the sea and the wide green of the woods. I look at it most nights. I know better, but I can't help imagining it: the most beautiful place on earth.

And then one day Thea, in one of her unsettling strokes of insight, calls it.

"I could take care of Dad," she says. "If you needed to go. You could move to the city, or wherever else. Start sophomore year out of state."

I look at her.

"I'm not going anywhere," I say. But we both know it's a lie.

I have outgrown this place. I love it and want so desperately for it to still belong to me, but it doesn't fit me anymore. The point of the Shire, contrary to what Elias says about the Orcs, is that, even when you get back to it, in your heart it's already gone. And the more time that passes, the more you feel it, and the more you itch—now that you've seen magic—to follow it.

Chapter 28

SAINT EIA, THE STORY GOES, STOOD AT THE edge of the ocean, empty and trapped against the sea, until a leaf grew to fit her and carry her across it. I suppose she had a mermaid destiny too.

When the dust cleared, she had found her faith, but at a cost. The falling-apart world was too disordered, too dangerous, for her to ever find her way home again. She lived the rest of her days in a distant country, among people who spoke a different language, and she never saw her faeries or the strong women of her tribe or her warrior goddesses again.

I wonder sometimes if her God was enough to compensate her for the loss of all those things. And I guess I will never know. I guess not knowing is the point. All I know is that if nature isn't God telling us a story about what God is, then God is nothing I can picture.

The morning I leave, I put my suitcase into Thea's messy car. My dad is at work and we both know he'd never say yes. I love him, but I do not agree with him. And he can't protect me from what's coming. I'm the one who has to protect things now.

Once I was a Loch Ness Monster on a bike, left behind and angry and wild. Then I was what everyone wanted me to be. Now I am a girl on a leaf. This world doesn't belong to the Father Jameses. It belongs to me. To Elias and Sister Suzanne and Barney and Gabe and me.

All the money I have saved from the convent has gone into a ticket and some money to live on once I'm there. I've bought a round trip, but with any luck, I won't be back anytime soon.

I take my passport out of the top drawer. I've spent months getting it, half intending not to use it.

I listen outside Gabe's door while he sleeps.

It is the Gabes I will let down if I do not find out how to be brave.

At Newark Airport, still under renovations after the flood, Thea gets out of the car and we hug.

She takes a selfie of us. I still look like Gollum.

She cries. I watch her drive away, trembling.

It's my first time in an airport. It's my first time on a plane. It's my first time flying over the ocean. It's my first time seeing what the clouds look like from the top down.

And somehow the scariest thing is, will Elias be there? And if he is, will he still want me there too?

The journey takes three days, from a plane to a bus to a boat. To get to the secret beach, you first have to get to Shark Bay. From there it's a three-hour drive, followed by a hike down a long dirt track to the shore. Even then, you have farther to go by boat. It terrifies me. Me, a speck on the surface of the continent of Australia, very small, very foolish—far from home and desperately in love with someone who might break my heart.

When we dock, I'm surprised that the beach is exactly what Elias described. It's the greenest and most beautiful

237

place I've ever seen. It's the Garden of Eden, if any place is. It is a tiny place to try to protect, but also a perfect one. It is a place to begin.

There are cabins far back from the water's edge, in the tall grass. The dunes rise and fall like waves, so small against the sea. He's clustered in a group of people, planting what looks to be a never-ending expanse of reeds. There's only so much one person can do.

I step unsteady into the warm, shallow water where we land.

He stands up, half hidden by shade. I can't see his face, but then his arms fly up in the air. I walk toward him. And then he tackles me.

This is where we'll start.

We will shout our shitty anger.

We will make our stand.

We will stumble forward, not because we're certain but because reaching ahead is all that we can do.

We will try, even though we don't know how it ends.

Acknowledgments

I am lucky enough to work with the two most wonderful Rosemarys in the world: my editor, Rosemary Brosnan, and my agent, Rosemary Stimola. I could not have gotten through this story without their wisdom, inspiration, and support. I'm deeply indebted to Melanie Breakspear, Steve Dinan, Robyn Hughes, Ben Johnson, Georgina Kamsika, and ABM Nasir for their insights and generosity of spirit. Thank you to Courtney Stevenson, Martha Schwartz, and Kathryn Silsand for their guidance and thoughtfulness.

I am grateful to Tina Mueller and all the Mueller family for making work possible for me in 2020. Thank you to Pia Arrendell and to Pastor Sara for bringing much light to Cassie's journey. Thank you to Mark, whose faith in me keeps me moving forward.

I hesitated to write about insomnia because talking about insomnia breeds insomnia. But Cassie's sleeplessness was a big part of what inspired this story, and I'll take this opportunity to mention Sasha Stephens and her book *The Effortless Sleep Method* to set my karma right again.

Because I only get to see them long after a book is finished, I don't lavish nearly enough praise on Andrea Pappenheimer, Kathy Faber, Patty Rosati, and Jenny Sheridan. I am incredibly fortunate to have you all in my corner, and you always make me feel so at home.

Finally, I want to thank my mom for nurturing the warrior queen on a bike I used to be, and for showing me what it is to be brave.